MOUNTAIN LION AND BOBCAT

APEX INVESTIGATIONS: BOOK THREE

JULIA TALBOT

Julia Talbot

 Created with Vellum

CONTENTS

Mountain Lion and Bobcat

James Pearson is sick of being down and out. The Apex tech guru has been in a wheelchair since a client gone bad poisoned him, and he's determined to find out who's behind their run of seriously bad luck. He's also dreaming of a certain bobcat shifter, and he can't figure out if Hank was real, or if he was just a figment of James' fevered imagination.

Hank DeLong wants to leave undercover work behind him, and he's missing the connection he felt with James when he was working with Apex Investigations. So when he gets the chance to go back and help the PI firm figure out how all of their recent issues are connected, he jumps at the chance.

Not only do Hank and James have to deal with the mate bond they can feel forming, they also have to fight the danger lurking around every corner for the team. Can they heal James and bring all the threads together before someone gets killed?

Apex Investigations Reading Order

Fox and Wolf

Jaguar and Grizzly

Mountain Lion and Bobcat

Alpha and Bear

To Jaymi, who has encouraged me all the way with this series, to all the readers who have given me my confidence back and, as always, to my wife, BA.

PROLOGUE

Mick stood in the doorway to the command center and watched his only current resident kitty shifter, James, wheel around in his high-tech wheelchair. Nothing motorized for James, but it was sleek and racer style.

A frown tugged at his lips, but he pushed it back to neutral. James wouldn't thank him for pity. Or for sympathy to be honest. Hell, James would barely talk to him these days. Or anyone else but maybe Rey. That little fox was impossible to resist.

James had always been his independent one, the one who stayed in his own apartment over on Colfax, who didn't want Mick up in his business. Now the man slept in the office, only going to his apartment upstairs to bathe and eat once every couple of days.

He never ate with the guys anymore.

Maybe Mick should call Brock and Griz back in. James and jaguar shifter Brock were brothers in kittyhood, and he thought James missed his friend. Whether they were fighting like they did sometimes, or being all solidarity when times got bad, James and Brock were solid.

"Are you gonna stare at me all day, boss?" James finally glanced up at him, proving he knew Mick was there.

"Maybe. I pay the rent," Mick teased.

"Uh-huh."

He gritted his teeth against the need to shake James into talking to him instead of spitting out one-word answers. "Working on Dylan's industrial espionage case?" Dylan and Rey had taken a leave of absence for a few weeks, but Mick was glad his wolf packmate Dylan couldn't stand to be away from work for too long.

"Finished it this morning." James gave him a sideways glance. "You know what I'm working on."

"Making connections." Their last two major cases had been disasters, the last leaving James in this damn wheelchair until he healed. He would, Mick knew he would, but he hadn't just been injured. He'd been given some kind of poisonous substance that had put him down for weeks.

"Yeah. Weasels and cultists and tigers, oh my." James scowled at his big screen, which spanned three computers. "There has to be more, but there's just so many gaps. Whispers."

Damn. James was obsessed, and if he hadn't come up with more by now... "What does Rey think?" Rey was an information gatherer. He had ways of making connections.

James finally turned to face him fully. "That I need to find that ex-cop. Hank. The one Brock knows."

Mick frowned over. "Why? What does he know that you don't?"

Or was it just that the cop could do legwork where James was stuck inside.

"Rey says he was working the same case, just from a

different angle. Undercover. I don't remember much from when he was here."

"Didn't he leave you a card? I thought you two might... keep in touch."

"I don't know where it went." James sighed. "I need to talk to him. Maybe he can connect some dots." James looked at him, hope a terrible light in his golden eyes. "Can you find him for me?"

"Yeah. Yeah, kiddo." Anything to keep James with them, keep that excitement going. He hadn't seen James smile in ages. "No problem."

"Thank you. He'll have to come here. I won't leave."

No. No, he knew that.

"I'll get him reeled in." He had a way to message Brock. That jaguar of theirs would know how to find Hank. If he didn't, well, Mick would contact his friend on the force and call in a favor.

Whatever he needed to do to keep James with them and living.

"Thanks, boss."

"Come have some pizza with me and Kit," he asked, trying not to wheedle. They missed James even if he was right there.

"I've got work to do, boss. Maybe tomorrow, hmm? Maybe when I've—"

Kit came bustling in, pizza boxes in hand. "I brought us pepperoni!"

"Good man! That way we can all eat in here while we work."

James gave them both a knowing kind of glare, but then relented. "It smells good, little bear."

No one could resist Kit. No one.

"It does. Rey and Dylan are bringing the Cokes up."

James sighed, rolling his eyes dramatically, but looking more engaged than he had in weeks. "I'll put you all to work."

"Promise?" Kit spread out plates and napkins and pizza boxes.

"Yes, butthead bear. I'll make you look at spreadsheets."

"I'm good at that. And Mick can look at pictures like the big dork he is."

"Very funny, brat." Mick flicked Kit's ear.

Kit blushed and ducked his head, the sweet bear all grins.

Mick glared at James when he snorted, and James gave him a patently false innocent look.

Dylan and Rey saved the butthead from retribution, piling into the room with drinks and bags of chips. "Salty snacks and fizzy stuff!" Rey said. "As demanded by the bear."

James snorted, but he was there, present and interacting with them, and Mick wasn't about to look a gift kitty in the mouth.

This was his team. He would do anything for them.

ONE

Hank Delong wanted to eat a giant hamburger, drink an entire bottle of Fireball, and sleep for two years. In that order.

Too bad he was still undercover. Still looking for the head of the damn drug ring he thought he'd shut down when Stefan Hetrick went to jail after the thing with Apex Investigations. The damn drug organization was like a hydra. Get rid of one head, and another sprang up.

Jesus, he was tired.

He shoved his hands into his jacket pockets, the weather in Denver getting chilly. He loved the cold in his other form, which was a hairy bobcat, but like this? He was feeling the weather these days. Down to the bone.

He checked the address he'd been sent by a contact, hoping something came of this. Cocaine. Synthetic drugs called Peaches, for fuck's sake, and a cult that wouldn't seem to die? How did no one know who was behind it all?

He waited outside the club, the music inside banging loud, making his heart throb with it. And his head. He needed some rest; he was getting undercover burn out. Doing it for the cops was bad enough, but a joint task force for the DEA and FBI was relentless.

About three minutes later a van pulled up, nondescript and white. No window. Just about the time he was staring at it, his brain twitching into danger mode, two big guys in pantyhose masks jumped out.

No fucking way. No way.

The bigger guy moved fast—lightning fast, if he was honest—and grabbed him before he could reach for his piece.

Not that he needed to draw down on a city street. No one even shouted or gasped. He was tossed into the van and sat on, the air whooshing out of him, and no one would ever even know he was gone.

"Drive, Dylan. We don't want anyone suspecting we got him."

The huge beast sitting on him chuckled. "Hey, Hank. We brought you a bacon cheeseburger."

"Kit?" Surely that was Kit, who he'd met earlier in the year. "Can't breathe."

"Oh, dude!" Kit moved off him, peeling off the mask. "Sorry."

Mick pulled his mask off too. "Want a beer?"

Hank blinked. He might just short out. What the hell?

"I'm on duty."

"Well, we kinda made a deal with your supervisor. No blowing your cover, and we can steal you for a bit. So have a beer. You're hiding out with us."

"Can you do that?"

Mick's smile was pure lupine joy. "I sure can. I have contacts."

"Well, shit. Give me a beer." He had no idea if this was on the up and up, but fuck it. It was enforced rest, and he liked these guys.

Mick passed over a Fat Tire and Kit handed him a bacon

double cheeseburger that smelled like heaven. His mouth full on watered, and he pulled out that and the fries, which looked crisp and salty. His favorite.

"I owe you guys. Which I guess is the idea."

"James needed to see you. This was the safest way." Dylan waved from the driver's seat. "Hey, man."

"Hey. How, uh, how is James?" He'd really dug James, or at least he thought he had. Maybe it had all been a drug-fueled mess. They'd recuperated together for a bit after an attack on him and some of the team Mick led had been attacked.

"Sad. Worried. Stressed out." Kit looked so down in the mouth.

Me too. "Oh, well, that sucks." Hank gnawed his burger. "What does he need me for?"

"Information? Blow jobs? I don't know, man. I don't care." Mick growled softly. "Seriously. He perked up when he talked about you."

"Hey, I'm cool with that. I wasn't making progress on the case anyway." He grimaced. Maybe he was too long in the tooth for undercover work. No one trusted anyone these days, and in the organization he was infiltrating, it was worse than anywhere he'd ever been, even a real drug cartel. This was so... scattered. Too diverse somehow. No one knew what they were doing.

It was like a fucking web, and the spider was so big no one could see it crouching at the top eating flies.

"Good deal." Mick was worried. He could read it in the new lines on the man's face. Mick was fanatically protective of his team, and damned if Hank wouldn't help with whatever James needed.

They'd done him solid last time.

"Eat, man. You're safe. I've got an apartment for you with a good bed and unlimited hot water."

"Oh." That almost gave him a boner. The thought of

sleeping until he woke up, as safely as anyone could offer him, was the most amazing thing. "That sounds good." He ate, then licked all the salt and grease off his fingers, to boot.

"Man needs a break every so often, bud." Mick rumbled softly. "Even if he has to do it with a pack around him."

A pack. Yeah, he was used to being a loner. Bobcat shifter, after all. They were relatively solitary.

Kit flashed him this happy grin. "Mick collects people."

"I've heard that. I'll deal with it." He winked at Kit. Hell, he was curious to see James.

"Cool. Man, I could use a nap."

Dylan snorted up front. "Bears. Always napping."

"It's our super-power. Sleep." Kit made snoring noises.

"Hey, us big cats can snooze." He patted his belly. "And now I'm full and ready." Was this his life? Thank God, because he'd been about to lose it.

"We'll be home soon. Six minutes." Dylan hit the right turn signal.

"Are we on a timer?"

Mick shook his head, "Nope, but we need to make sure no one saw us or followed us."

Ah, yes. The pack alpha had taken a few hard blows to his pack in the past year, and would want to protect headquarters.

"I'm low on pay scale for that." Hank shrugged.

"You never know," Mick shot back. "We never thought anyone would come after us. We're just a gumshoe PI agency."

"Then we got noticed." Kit rolled his eyes. "Rey was worth it."

"He is," Dylan said it softly, but his tone was proud.

"Yeah. I get that. Sometimes you meet someone who's important." It had happened to him, once or twice.

"That you do." Dylan chuckled. "Never expected him to be a fox."

"How do you keep from eating him?"

"Mmm. I channel the hunger into something else."

"Ew!" Kit laughed uproariously. "TMI."

"Yep." Mick rolled his eyes. "Anyway, you can crash for a bit, then consult with James."

"Sounds like a fucking plan, Mick. I'm beat."

"Excellent." They pulled into the underground garage, the heavy door closing behind them. This was new, he thought. Maybe not, because half his time at Apex had been spent unconscious, but he had a feeling Mick had made more improvements.

"Soon this place will be like the bat cave," Hank said.

Mick rolled his eyes. "Yeah, yeah. We've been invaded twice. I need to find new ways to keep us safe."

"That's what James is working toward," Kit muttered. "He's going to make himself nuts."

"Ah. Well, I'll do what I can, of course." Privately, he thought Mick was making himself nuts. But hey, who was he to judge? He couldn't walk down the street without waiting for someone to shoot him in the back.

Whatever. He needed to rest and then he'd go see the cougar, see what was what.

Sleep. In a bed.

That was a hell of a prospect. After a shower, that was the first thing he was gonna do.

Two

Hank was never going to wake up.

James Pearson told himself to be patient. He had to be, but...

James paced as well as anyone could in a wheelchair. Three strokes of the wheel in one direction. Three in the other. That was all the space he had if he wanted to turn at the end of each rush.

He could go up there and wake Hank up. Maybe take him one of the frozen sausage biscuits Kit always stocked in the main fridge. James was starting to get... antsy.

His phone rang, Brock's face popping up, and he grabbed it. "Brother."

"Stop stressing."

James blinked. No way. No way did Brock know that about him right at this very moment. They were close as brothers, but there was no psychic bullshit. "What are you talking about?"

He left off the 'butthead'.

"I know you. You're freaking out. You need to breathe and

do the next thing." Brock's light Portuguese accent always soothed him. "What is the next thing?"

"I want to talk to the undercover guy. I want to know what he knows." James wanted to look the man in the eyes and see if he was crazy because he kept dreaming about the hot son of a bitch.

"He'll wake up soon. Maybe try luring him out with food." Brock chuckled. "We're not as food focused as the bears, but we all have favorites."

"Mick says he's in bad shape."

"As bad as you?" Brock teased, but there was an underlying edge to it. They could fight as well as they could kitty snuggle.

Oh, he was going to bite Brock. Hard. As soon as they were in the same room. "Asshole."

"What? I have PTSD. I'm hiding. At least you're trying to work it out." The admiration in Brock's voice was real, and it warmed him.

"I have to. If I stop—"

"I know, *irmão*. Do you want to come here?"

"No. No, you and Griz are bonding. I would never interrupt that. And Mick is so freaked out already..." Mick was good to everyone and deserved some love too.

"Then do your thing. If you need me, I'm here. Take the bobcat a steak."

"A steak, huh? Baked potato, no salad?" Kit would make that happen for him.

"Steak fries. Salty. And garlic bread instead of dessert."

"Right on. Thanks, brother. I miss you."

"Ditto. I'll be home soon-ish. I swear." Brock never swore on something he didn't mean.

James just didn't know if Brock's definition of soon was the same as his. Brazilians had their own time clock sometimes.

He hung up with Brock, then hit the intercom to Kit's office. Hmm. No answer, so he called up to Kit's apartment.

"Yes?" Kit was singing; he could hear the Taylor Swift playing in the background.

"Are you shaking it off, baby bear?" He chuckled at the thought of Kit wiggling it to that song.

"Possibly. What's up?"

"I need help. Like steak and salty steak fries help. With garlic bread."

Kit paused. "You want to cook it or order it?"

"Order." He didn't cook. "Two. For the new guy and me."

"Okay. I know the best place, and it will get here hot and yummy. Rare?" Kit was the absolute best.

"You rock. Get for everyone and I'll buy?"

"You bet. You gonna be all private with the bobcat, or are we all eating together?" Kit teased.

"I'm going to be private, but I'd like to have dessert later, all of us? Maybe?" Hank might not want sweets, but the wolves and bear would. So would Rey.

"That sounds fab. They have a great cheesecake. All different levels of sweet. Plain for you and Hank, right?"

"Right, sweet bear. Thank you. Seriously. You're the best."

"No problem. Love you." Kit hung up, leaving him just sitting there for a moment. He hoped Kit never lost that sweetness.

He hoped, one day, he'd find a little of his own deep inside somewhere.

He shook his head. Okay, until the steak came, he needed to work. Then he would seduce the bobcat to work with him with seared meat. Salt too. Always worked on him.

He chuckled at his own nonsense, wheeling back to his computer. Rey came into the office, two cups of coffee in his hands.

"What's funny?"

"Oh, nothing." James smiled at Rey when he handed over a coffee. He had a real fondness for the little fox shifter. "What are you up to?"

"I came to do a little work—research for one of the clients. Want to hang out?"

"I do. Until the steaks come." Rey gave him a surprised look. "I'm tempting the bobcat," James said.

"Ooh. That sounds fun. Are you going to sit outside his door and waft the steaky-smell under his door?"

"Nope. I'm gonna wheel right up and knock. Brock says steak, and I need him to wake up and work with me." He was being selfish, and he knew it, but there it was. James figured without him, Hank wouldn't have slept at all.

"He'll like it. You two got along great before, right?"

He shrugged. "I don't remember. We slept a lot. Drugs."

"Oh. Oh!" Rey gave him tilty head. "Well, I do. I mean, you guys were like a house afire."

"We were?" He took the coffee and drank deep. "Can I tell you a secret?"

"Of course. Dork."

He rolled his eyes, but he laughed, didn't he? "I dream about him."

"No shit?" Rey bounced closer, eyes wide. "So like, you want to know if you're dreaming about him or someone random who just looks like him in your dreams?"

"I knew you would get it." Rey was a giant derp. Just like him.

"I do. I mean, I have to go on faith sometimes after finding out there are dire crocodile shifters..."

James rolled his eyes. "What can I help you and Dylan with, man? Until the steak gets here."

"You aren't into dreams, then? I mean, they're not interesting to you?" Rey watched him carefully, copper eyes curious.

"Huh? Oh, sure." James said it casually, because he couldn't let Rey know how intense these dreams were.

They were sweaty kinds of dreams. Deep, hot, squirmy dreams.

Rey looked at him, his expression quick and too sharp for his own good.

He ducked his head. Hiding. "Anyway. I need to pass the time too." James had no idea how long steaks would take. "You two are the only ones on a case."

"Yeah. It's nothing fun. Just some research into financial records. There's a company stealing from their contractors, and I'm following the money."

"That sucks. Thank God Mick is honest to a fault."

Rey nodded, settling into a chair and slipping on a headset. "Can you backtrack this supplier link?"

"I bet I can. You're working the bank accounts?" James winked over.

"You know it, man. I'm relentless."

"It's one of my favorite things about you, foxy."

"Yep. S'why I love you, brother lion." Rey had learned that brother stuff from Brock, just like he had. It was comforting and helped them all bond. That was Mick and his whole pack thing.

He loved them all so much and he had to find a way to figure out who had come after them and why. So he needed Hank to get up and get moving. Now.

God, his tail was lashing with frustration, and he wasn't even fuzzy.

"Stop. Kit will bring food, and that will get him out."

James laughed. "Sorry."

They worked about twenty minutes, and Kit appeared just about the time he was going to call. "Hot and amazing with a lovely sear. Not steamed a bit. Go get him, kitty."

"Will do." He stacked the two boxes on his lap and headed

carefully out to Hank's newly assigned apartment. He breathed deep, the hair on the back of his neck twitching. Hank was just this weird, shadowy figure for him now, and he needed to figure out why.

He knocked on the door, telling himself that it was his right.

"Just a mo'," came the quick reply. The voice was groggy, but familiar, and butterflies swarmed in his belly.

He heard it in his dreams every night.

The door opened, Hank standing there, dark gold hair everywhere, chest bare, sweats hanging low on his hips. "Oh! Hey. James."

"Hank. I brought—" *Me.* "—food."

Christ, lion. Get it together.

"Yeah?" That stubby nose quivered, wrinkling up. Then Hank's eyes went wide. "Oh, fuck, did you bring me a steak?"

"Yeah. Steak and fries. Rare. With a side of garlic bread." He tried to smile, but it didn't feel like it worked. "Can I come in?"

"Shit, yeah. Yeah, sorry. Hey, I got Cokes and beer that Kit left for me. Which one do you want?" Hank turned on a light on the way back into the apartment.

"A Coke is fine, thank you." He wheeled into the living area and put the food on the coffee table, sitting back after and catching his breath. This whole wheelchair thing was harder than you'd think, honestly.

"Got it." Hank brought two Cokes, then hesitated. "Am I underdressed?"

"No. Eat while it's hot."

"Oh, good deal." Hank opened the vented box. "Look at that. Homemade steak sauce."

"Smells good, hmm?"

God, he couldn't stop staring. Hank fascinated him, drew

him like nothing he'd ever known, and that wide, bare chest made his hands itch.

"Yeah. It's amazing. You're eating with me, right?" Hank hovered over the steak, glancing up at him, eyes greenish gold and flashing in the low light.

"Yes. Yes, of course. Sorry. I was just resting a second." He set his brakes and leaned forward to take his box, fighting not to overbalance. Don't. Not here. Not in front of this man.

"No worries. I just hate to be rude. You guys gave me my best sleep in—" Hank bit back the words. "A long time."

"No worries. You deserved it. Thank you for coming out." He snagged the box and balanced it on his legs. "I appreciate it."

Was that weird?

It might be weird.

It was probably weird.

"Well, you did have me kidnapped." Hank winked, the relaxed, easy expression never changing. "That's good steak. Totally worth it."

"I did. It's a thing. Kidnapping." Gods, James! Shut. Up.

"Apparently your team does it all the time." Hank nibbled another bite of steak, making sex noises.

He ate a bite of steak, not even tasting it, because he was so focused on those sounds. Hank caught him, fascinated him, and he couldn't even pretend to not stare.

"Do I have sauce on my chin?" Hank asked, but those pupils had dilated, Hank staring right back.

"N-no. No. Your chin is—" Utterly lickable. "—fine."

"Cool. Eat with me, man. I hate to eat alone." Hank licked his fingers after nipping up a fry.

He nodded and ate a bit of fries, trying to think of something to say, but he simply couldn't. It was enough to sit here and watch.

Hank smiled at him, the expression lighting up his face. "Come over here? Can you scoot in next to me?"

"I—Do you mind? I lost my back end. At least for now. They say it was the poison."

"Yeah. I was down for a bit. Come on over. Want me to hold your box?"

"Please." He handed it over and tried to slide, nice and smooth, over to the sofa. Of course, that didn't work, did it?

No, he ended up with the chair tilting on him, and he clung to the side of the sofa, the damn thing on top of him.

Excellent.

"I got you." Hank was up in a heartbeat, food on the table, lifting him gently and putting him down on the couch, where they tumbled together a little. "Oof. Sorry."

"Uh-huh." Where was the hole that was going to open up and swallow him? "I'm sorry. That was..." Not cool.

"There you go." Hank got them settled, a little closer than he expected, then fed him a fry. "They're so good while they're hot, man. Come on."

His lips brushed Hank's fingertips, and he swore he could feel the rush of electricity between them. Hell, it was possible they made a visible spark.

Grunting, Hank took a deep breath. "See? Good."

"Uh-huh. Really." Whoa. Fuck him. That was pure lightning.

Hank cleared his throat. "Uh, so did you want to tell me why you had me cat napped?"

"I needed to talk with you. See what you know. Share what I know." *See if you're dreaming about me too.*

"About the drug case?" Hank shook his head. "Not sure I know a lot."

"Oh. Well, I— Me either." James sighed. No. Hank didn't dream about him. "Maybe when you're ready, I can show you my research..."

"I would love that. I missed your face."

Something in Hank's voice caught him. Maybe Hank hadn't dreamed of him because he remembered some of what happened.

"I—I missed—I have dreams about you." Oh, James. Shut up.

"You do?" He could see Hank weighing whether to make it funny or not. All the emotions chased each other, then Hank licked his lips. "What kind?"

James felt his entire body flush hot. "I— Uh. Dreams."

"Sweaty kind or eek a serial killer kind?" Hank wasn't joking, not really. That gaze never wavered, holding James right there.

"I'm not scared of you. Not even a little bit." He was intrigued. Aroused. Hungry.

"Oh, good." Hank sat back just enough to eat, clearly unwilling to waste the steak. "That would suck."

"Yeah. Yeah, it would." He ate another fry. They were good. Better now than they were a few minutes ago.

Salty was his thing.

"Anyway, I have permission from on high to hang and help you out, so I'll do my best." Hank touched his wrist for a moment in between bites.

He felt the contact all the way up his arms, and his fingers curled. "I appreciate it. I need help figuring this out."

"You have a good team. This has to be bigger than anyone thinks."

James read between the lines there. "The cops think we're serious amateurs. Like how can anyone fuck up as much as we have?"

Hank gave him a wry look. "The cops, the feds. I know Brock, though. He's no fool, so you guys have either had the worst run of luck ever, or there's a Moriarty to Sherlock level of conspiracy going on here."

"I think it's a little bit of both, but I think we're being targeted. Just us, specifically, and it started with Rey." He knew Rey was a victim too, but he couldn't deny the coincidence.

"You mean when he came to the agency?"

James jerked his chin in agreement. "He was a client first. One of his own clients got killed. The guy who did it came after him." Shit had, immediately, gone downhill. Weregators, for fuck's sake. Who dealt with those?

"Huh. Okay, well, I can look into him as it won't step on toes. What about the guy who killed his client?"

"Tiger shifter named Patel. He's in jail right now."

Hank moved against him, elbow brushing his ribs. "And no one has gotten him out?"

"Nope. Says he's safer there."

"Interesting. I might be able to work that angle." Hank licked salt off his lips.

"Your drug guy Hetrick says the same thing." Again, James didn't believe in coincidence.

From the look in Hank's eyes, neither did the cop.

"I've been trying to convince the brass that this was a huge net operation beyond the drugs for ages," Hank said before munching his last bites. "They keep telling me it's too disconnected, but it's there, just like a spiderweb before the sun hits it."

James nodded. "Or before you walk into it face first. There's trouble. I don't know how to put the pieces together yet, but I will."

"I'll help." Hank patted his flat belly. "Thanks for the steak. Do I owe you?"

"I expensed it." James winked, feeling more on even ground. He pushed the rest of his steak over. "Here. Finish it."

"Thanks. You eat the fries though." Hank fed him another fry, and he thought that touch lingered on his lips.

"Thank you." Whoa. His voice was husky as shit.

"You're welcome." Hank was right there with him. Those eyes had gone hot.

"I—" His fingers itched with needing to touch.

"Um. So am I supposed to be doing anything else?"

"Dessert with the guys, in a bit." He smiled and got ready to move, pushing over to the edge of the sofa and balancing himself on the arms of his chair. "About seven. You're welcome to come."

He got his butt in the chair this time without falling. "Thanks for sharing supper with me." He hadn't gotten any information, but he'd...eaten?

"You don't have to leave..." Hank stood, walking him to the door. "Or I could come work with you some."

"I have a whiteboard and stuff in my apartment, if you want to see."

"I do." Hank bounced up on his toes. "Oh. If we're meeting for dessert I should put on a shirt, at least. What's the shoe policy? Can I get away with socks?"

"Totally. Everyone tends to get furry."

"Oh. Really?" Something like bare need flashed on Hank's face. "I haven't shifted just because in—a long time."

"This is a safe space. You can shift here, be yourself." With me. Be yourself with me. Hank even made James want to be with the rest of the team.

"Can you shift right now?" Hank nodded at the chair, his voice cautiously curious.

"You mean right this second?"

"No. I'm sorry, I meant with your injury." Hank grinned wryly. "Words are my friends."

"I hear you. I can. I can't use my back legs very well, so I just don't." He refused to blush. Refused to.

"Oh." Hank's face fell. "It's nice to have another cat. For snuggling."

"It is. Brock left. I snuggled with him. I could...I just..." He snapped his lips closed. "Why do you make me so stupid?"

"I don't know." Hank put a hand on his shoulder. "It's mutual. Maybe it's our shared drug experience."

He panted hard, the touch like lightning along his spine. "Maybe. Can you feel that?"

"The lightning in a bottle? Yeah. Boom." Hank stroked his hair. "Can we figure it out over the next little while? I can stay a few... weeks maybe, even."

"Sure. I'm not going anywhere." He smiled at Hank, nodded. Whatever this was, it wasn't real. It was drugs. "Well, I'm going to my apartment. I'm in number four. If you want, I'll be there. Otherwise seven p.m. in the common area. There's cheesecake."

"I'll get a shirt on and come to yours. If that's cool. I bet it's more comfy to you." Hank opened the door for him. "Hey."

"What?"

Hank waited until he rolled out the door. "It's not just drugs." Then Hank closed the door behind him.

––––––––

Hank headed to James' apartment once he was actually dressed in jeans, socks and a shirt someone had obviously loaned him.

Possibly a bear, as big as it was.

He should probably just go to dessert, but the disappointment on James' face was tugging him right back into the man's orbit. So he found number four and knocked.

"Come in, Hank." The door buzzed and clicked open.

"Thanks." He immediately checked his danger areas out of habit, then stopped to look around. Nice. Sleek. Maybe more modern than he expected. And the whiteboard and pin type bulletin board... god it was huge and covered in pictures and string. "That's...intense."

"It's what I do." James had pictures of some suspects he knew, some that he'd never heard of.

Hank walked over to look at it closely, tracing the lines that radiated out from the tiger, Patel. Gatorcroc shifters. Rey and his dead client. A flash drive with files. A still from a video with Patel holding a gun. Then there were the ferrets, Mr. Hetrick and his wife. Of course, there was a line from the wife to a picture of him...

"Yeah, not one of my proudest undercover moments."

James snorted. "You don't usually toss yourself into the flames for your job?"

"Not like that, no." The lady wolf had been sad and lonely and a little nuts. Maybe it was the synthetic drug they called peaches. Maybe it was the cult. Who knew?

"Yeah, Brock told me all about your...undercover work." James managed to say that with a straight face.

Hank stuck out his tongue. "Don't be a bitchy kitty. It was in the name of busting a drug ring. Or a cult, which I didn't even know about until you. It really is Sherlock in its ridiculousness."

James crowed. "So you did mean the BBC show! Are you a fan?"

"I was until season four." He was still wounded. That whole season just needed to not exist.

"Yeah. That was a disappointment, but you're right. I think there's a Moriarty. I just don't know who the Sherlock Holmes is."

"Me either. Can't be Rey, right? I mean, you said he brought it with him, but he was pretty clueless."

He looked at the pictures of Brock and Locke, Rey and Dylan. "Where are the pictures of Mick and Kit? You?"

"I don't belong on this board." James sounded purely affronted.

"No? They poisoned your desk. You specifically. Why?" Hank liked the thoroughness of James' pattern, but James and Mick belonged on there for sure. Kit he had no idea about. He seemed... adorable.

"Did they know it was me? I assumed they wanted Rey."

"Yeah? Because of what? He was sharing your office?" His gaze fastened on the picture of the fox shifter, who just looked so small and unassuming and copper.

"Yes. It started with him, but I know he's a victim. I know it. Dylan is his mate. He's one of us."

"He is." Hank chewed his lower lip. "You need the rest up here. Kit and Mick and you. Your admin. Carrie?"

"She's not involved. She can't be."

"You're too close to make that call, man. You know that." Hank didn't think that they were involved either, but they had to be considered. "If nothing else, we have to tie in those strings. See if there's a connection you haven't seen."

He moved closer to James because he had to, the weird spark between them drawing him right over.

"You're just mad that you're already up here." James winked at him, but he rolled over to a desk and searched through a file folder.

"Well, the fact that you only linked me to the lady wolf? Yeah. I mean, I worked with Brock and Locke more than once. And I was with you for what? Weeks?"

"Was it that long? It was a fantasy, this amazing thing I can barely remember."

"I think so." Hank touched James' shoulders. "I'm not just a fever dream. I—I liked being with you."

James' head fell forward. "I can't stop dreaming of you. I don't understand. I needed you to come so I could see you."

Hank leaned down, lips next to James' ear. "Are you disappointed?"

"In you? Never."

"Good." He saw James shiver as he spoke, his breath fanning James' skin.

"I—Whoa." James looked up at him, green eyes bright.

He wanted to kiss that mouth. The urge was sudden, but not really shocking. Just... strong.

Hank bent a little more, but a knock on the door had him popping up so fast he almost fell over.

James shuddered softly, turning his head to look at a monitor.

"You ready for cheesecake?" Kit called.

James shook his head, but said, "Sure, honey."

"We'll come back here after, huh?" He stroked the back of James' neck.

"If your cat isn't horrified by mine." James leaned back into the touch.

"No chance." Hank knew he would want to be near James, human or kitty. James called to his soul.

"Cake with cheese," he murmured. "Want me to push?"

"Do you mind? My hands are tied. Tired. They're tired."

"No problem at all." That way he got to stay close and look and sniff without stalking. He took the handles of the chair and began to walk James to the door. He turned James and opened the door right into Kit. "Hey, buddy."

"Mr. Hank. Hi again."

"Hey. You jonesing for some cheesecake?"

Kit gave him a sheepish look. "Yeah. The steak is nice, but I got plain for you and James, banana toffee for Mick and Dylan, and honey and berry for me and Rey. Carrie went home to her mom."

"She doesn't snuggle, huh?"

"I'm not sure she eats," James said. "I think she's a demon, not a shifter."

"James." Kit chortled, though.

"Maybe a lesser devil. It's very possible." James in teasing mode was the most adorable thing ever.

"That I could see. More like an imp who can pop in and out."

Hank snorted at them, following Kit down the hall to an elevator. "Are we going up or down?"

"Down two floors. Up is office. Down one is Mick and me. Down two is the common rooms." Kit beamed at them. "Thank you for coming to dessert."

"You're welcome." Hank let one hand stroke James' neck, just lightly, before grabbing the handles again. He loved how James leaned back toward his touch.

"James has been working so hard," Kit said. "We've missed his face."

"He's a bit obsessive is he?"

James snorted. "I prefer focused."

"A little nuts," Kit added cheerfully. "But that's what makes a good investigator. Even I forget to eat sometimes."

"But you never forget to nap." James was laughing out loud now.

When they reached what he remembered to be the big common lounge, hopeful faces turned toward them, smiles breaking out when Mick, Dylan, and Rey saw James.

"There they are!" Rey bounced over to hug Kit, then went on tiptoe to kiss Kit's cheek. "Can I hug you?" Rey asked Hank. "I'm a hugger."

"Sure." He opened his arms and had to oof when Rey grabbed him in a surprisingly strong hug.

"You're something else." He could see why James liked Rey. The fox was pure joy.

James' mountain lion on the other hand, was pure sex and need, and Hank wanted to bite him. Hard. He had no idea what parts of James worked, though, and didn't want to make the man feel worse than he did, so Hank would wing it, not take it too fast.

He wanted to know what was hurt, how bad it was, and then they'd work around it.

"We're so glad you both came. We've missed you, James." Rey went to kiss James on the cheek, so gentle.

Everyone was so careful with James.

Maybe James needed to exercise a little. To be bumped back into the fast lane sideways.

"Hey, kiddo," Mick said. "Come over with us. Kit got you a tart original."

"You like tarty types, huh?"

Mick snorted. "We've all heard things about your undercover life, Hank."

"Oh ho! No being nice to the new bloke, hmm?" He slapped Mick on the shoulder. "Thanks for the rest, though. I needed it."

"Worth getting kidnapped for?" Mick asked.

"Hell, the steak was worth that. So was that first cheeseburger. And the sleep. It's so good to see your friendly faces too." Hank stood next to James, who had parked his chair by a big recliner. "You want the chair?" Hank asked.

"No. No, I'll stay here, thanks."

"Okay cool." He plopped down next to James, wanting to be close. Then he reached out and took hand in his.

Kit grinned at him while serving up cheesecake. "Coffee, James?"

"No thank you. Is there milk?"

"There is."

"Oh, me too, please." Hank loved milk. Loved it. He could lap it out of a bowl. Or off James' skin.

James purred for him, deep and soft and low.

He squeezed those long fingers.

"Milk it is," Kit said. "Anyone else?"

"I'll take coffee," Rey said.

"Addict," Dylan teased.

"You have a point?" Rey laughed and leaped into Dylan's arms.

"Nope." Dylan took a kiss, and Hank had to look away to give them some privacy.

Fortunately looking away let him look at James, and that neat blond beard, the green eyes. Yum. There was something about James that really called to him. Not just the hot looks.

He knew what James meant. He dreamed too.

James squeezed his hand, then let go to eat his cheesecake. Hank felt that touch everywhere. Fucking everywhere. All the way up his arm.

He took a deep breath, trying to calm down his overheated body.

"You okay, man?" James asked. "You look stressed out."

"No, I'm good. I am." He was so good.

"Excellent." James grinned at him. "Enjoy your cheesecake."

"You too." *Please lick your fork. Please.*

James tilted his head, forehead wrinkling. Then he licked his fork.

Oh. Hank bit back a moan. That was just what he needed. James held his gaze, eyes hot and hungry.

He took a bite, but he didn't think he tasted it. Everything was James. Hank forked up another bite, offering it to those sweet lips, and James opened up.

Hank watched, all but holding his breath, as James nipped it off the fork.

"Yours is good too." James hummed, the sound rumbling in his chest.

"Yeah. Yeah, they're yummy." When he glanced away,

everyone was watching them, but they all managed to find something else to stare at.

He grinned. They had no room to talk, except Kit and Mick... He wasn't one hundred percent sure Kit's balls had dropped.

"Mmm." Kit moaned over his honey thing, and okay, maybe they had. That was a sex noise.

"Are we going to snuggle, Mick?" Rey asked. "It's been so long."

"Yeah. God, yeah. I miss you guys."

Hank stroked one finger down arm. "You're going to stay, right? Hang out?"

"Huh? Oh, I—"

"Come on, man. I'll help. You need some kitty time." He wanted to cuddle James specifically.

"For you."

Damn, those two words felt so good.

Hank beamed, and the guys all gave him the big smiles and thumbs up. "Thanks."

The creamy dessert tasted even better now.

They all finished up, then one by one started getting naked and shifting. It should have been weird, but it wasn't. "Need any help?" Hank asked.

James looked worried, uncomfortable, but the man trusted him enough to nod and reach for him. He helped James lift up to get off the sweats and socks, then the shirt. Kit arranged some pillows so he could lower James down with them. Then Hank stripped off, trying not to be self-conscious at the way James stared at him.

He didn't want to spring wood, either.

That was for later in their conversations. He had no doubt, but not in front of the guys. He laid down and pulled James gently to him.

James leaned into him and sighed, snuggling in, going

fuzzy immediately. Oh, so beautiful. That long, lean mountain lion body had the softest fur.

The smell of bear was strong, and Kit rolled up to James' back as Hank shifted, cuddling to James' belly.

Soon they were all there, grooming one another and snuggling in a puppy pile. Kit was a doll, but Mick surprised him with how sweet he was, how protective.

James nuzzled him, tongue rough on his whiskers.

His nose twitched, and he chuffed. That tickled.

James scooted closer, and he rowled happily. He loved the deep, rich scent of his cougar, the fuzzy belly. He explored lazily, letting his tongue drag over James' fur.

James huffed out a breath, curling around him a little. So warm. He loved to see the heavy tail, to feel the way James stretched, all the way to his toes.

That back end wanted to work just fine.

He hoped he could help with it.

Right now he focused on grooming and growling and rumbling. There was a lot of that going on, though he thought Rey was already asleep, and Dylan wasn't far behind. Kit was solid behind them, a block of heat.

His eyelids got heavy, his motions slowing. This was magic. James rubbed their cheeks together, sharing their scent. Yes. That made Hank's eyes cross.

Pretty kitty. James made him purr, and when the mountain lion groomed his whiskers, he melted.

Hank could just stay right here for days.

Mick chuffed softly and licked his ear, earning a playful bat.

James seemed so happy like this. He'd needed it.

Hank thought the contact was doing him some good too. Cats might be relatively solitary, but he had a human half too. Humans weren't meant to be alone. Kit's paw smelled like Fritos, and fascinated his tongue, while the little fox vibrated, even in rest. So busy. Dylan slept hard, deeply, and Mick watched over them.

James clearly wanted to sleep, but kept forcing himself awake, pushing his eyes open.

Hank licked James' whiskers, soothing him. *Sleep. Sleep. We're safe.* Okay, so James couldn't know what he was thinking, but he tried to help with his actions.

James yawned, going heavy against his belly.

Perfect. He just kept grooming and making deep rumbling noises. He felt it when his—when the mountain lion fell asleep, breathing deep against his chest.

That was when Hank allowed his eyes to close, let himself truly relax.

He'd never felt so safe. Never.

People could say what they wanted about this team being the bad luck shifters, but Hank knew something they didn't know. No matter what happened, these guys had each other's backs. And now he got the feeling they had his too.

Three

James had the worst headache. Seriously. He'd been staring at his screen as he'd been avoiding thinking about anything.

Not the case. Not the team. Not Hank. Definitely not Hank. Nope. Hank was...beautiful. Strong. Sexual. Tempting.

And he had no real reason to be there helping James. When he figured that out, he would leave.

The dreams weren't getting better. Not at all.

"Hey." Kit walked in, handing him a cup of coffee with lots of milk. "Hank still sleeping?"

"I guess. I haven't seen him. Thanks, honey."

"You're welcome." Kit bent to rub noses with him.

He smiled at his office mate, letting himself relax back in the chair a bit, breathe and close his eyes. Kit was always so sweet, so calming. Unless he was fighting. Lord. Then he was fierce.

Warm hands landed on his shoulders. "Your head hurts."

Hank knew. How did Hank know?

"I—yes. It does."

"You need to stop staring at that screen for a bit. Be analog. Print some shit our for us to look at it a different way." Hank began to massage his neck, thumbs rubbing in hard.

"Mnh?" Work? What? James moaned, his head falling forward.

"Mmhmm...You're tight as frozen rope, angel." Hank kissed his temple.

"Been working, is all."

"I know. I've been lazy as all fuck. Put me to work." Hank sat in the office chair next to him.

Oh, he missed those hands.

"I'm trying to discover what the connection between Rey and Mick is."

Hank tilted his head. "Pre Rey hiring you, you mean."

"Of course. There has to be a connection, doesn't there?" He needed there to be one.

"Okay. How far do we go back?" Hank looked around, then snagged a pen and notebook.

"Mick didn't know Rey. Rey found us online."

"One assumes Rey kept case files? Did you ever have clients in common?" Hank started scribbling bullet points.

"I did, and we didn't. Not that I've discovered, anyway. My clients like their privacy." Rey waved at Hank.

"Hey, Rey." Hank looked around. "Did we lose Kit?"

"He went to get snacks." Rey sat in his desk chair, then rolled over. "Have we looked at everyone else? Dylan when he was a cop? Brock's many other jobs?"

"I've got lists. Nothing yet."

"What about you, James?" Hank asked.

James blinked. "Me?"

"Yeah." Hank stared at him. "What did you do before this?"

"I taught at a university." His shoulders drew up, shame buzzing through him.

Hank's ears would be twitching if he was in cat form. Whiskers too, James would bet. "What happened?"

"I left." He didn't want to talk about it, not here.

"Oh." Hank sank back in his chair. "Well, we should cross-check your students."

"Yeah…I'm going to…" What? Run away?

"Hey." Hank touched him, and all his jangling nerves settled. "You know what I was doing a few months ago."

"I do. Come to my apartment?" Please, let me have my pride?

"Sure." Hank rose, smiling for Rey. "Enjoy the snacks."

"Kit will bring some by. Pizza rolls."

"Oh, I like those. Spicy goodness." He smiled at Rey, trying for relaxed, confident.

"Me too." Hank winked broadly. "Come on, angel."

Angel? Him? Bah. Yeah, come on.

Hank walked beside him, which was nice, though he would happily have stared at that taut butt.

They got to his place, Hank settling in on the couch in no time, looking all slinky and hot for such a bulky kitty.

James could lick him, top to bottom.

"Come sit with me, James?"

"I—" How was he supposed to do that and not touch?

Hank smiled and patted the couch. "Please. I know whatever you have to tell is hard."

James wheeled over so he could hoist himself to the couch, and Hank immediately pulled him in, one arm around him.

God, so warm. So fine. He purred softly.

"That's it. No need to be all tense. Just relax." Hank's breath fell on his cheek.

"You make that easy." He wanted to touch, so badly.

"Do I? Good." Hank kissed the corner of his lips. "Tell me and get it over with, and then we can nap."

"I was accused of being inappropriate with a student. Of

forcing him to do sexual acts with me for grades. It wasn't true. I never would. I don't even remember the kid being in my classes." And he'd been exonerated, but that hadn't mattered, had it? No. By then he was the prof who'd extorted sex. Gay sex at that.

Hank's golden gaze sharpened. "So who had it in for you?"

"His name was Gage. I don't talk about it. Mick brought me on, no questions asked. There's a lot of us here, with no questions asked. Brock introduced us, you know?"

"How did you know Brock?" Hank was a cop. He was good at asking the hard questions.

"He spoke in one of the seminars I went to. Investigative techniques. He was fascinating." They'd immediately become friends.

"Ah. He is good at that, for someone who hides behind a hoodie half the time, huh?" Hank chuckled. "Jaguar of many talents."

"He is. He's my soul brother." But he'd never craved Brock like he craved Hank. They were platonic and brotherly.

"He's a good guy. I hope we can be friends instead of just colleagues." Hank leaned on him, but didn't knock him over or anything. "You, on the other hand, make me want things."

"Do I?" He searched Hank's eyes. "I want more than things. I want you." He was broken, but he still needed.

"Good." Hank's smile was all cream licking cat.

"I'm not sure I work down there. I haven't jacked off since." It was only fair to warn Hank.

"We'll have to try, but there's no rush." Hank hugged him with that strong arm. "I'm still sleep deprived. Who knows what my body will do?"

"You smell like need. Need and heat." He didn't believe that Hank would have any problems. At all. The scent of him was all male and so musky.

"Yeah. I've been trying to keep my hands to myself. Not scare you off." Hank wiggled a little, and James thought the musky scent intensified.

"I'm not scared." Intrigued, yes. Scared, no.

"Good deal. Because you make me hard."

"Should we..." Because he wanted to. More importantly, his cat needed to touch, to explore. He ran one hand up along Hank's heavy bicep.

"Should we what?" Hank blinked, those long lashes blond, but darker at the tips. "We could get naked. Or I could, if you feel weird, not that I didn't see and admire yesterday..."

"I'm not ashamed. Scars mean you healed."

"That's it. You survived." Hank sat up to tug off his shirt, showing off that wide, hard chest and flat belly.

James reached out to touch, stroking Hank's abs, tracing the muscles, one at a time.

Hank shivered, those flat brown nipples drawing up, goosebumps rising on that golden skin. James purred and leaned close, tongue flicking out to tease.

"Mmm. Yeah." Hank put one hand behind his head, gentle, but holding him right there.

He smiled at the sound, letting his tongue flick out, over and over, the connection heady, the salt on Hank's skin just right.

Hank writhed for him, body undulating like a dancers. He hadn't expected that kind of flexibility, which was silly, because fellow cat, right? Hank just looked so solid.

So pretty. He let himself suck, pulling gently and steadily, tongue sliding over Hank's hard little nub.

"Damn. Oh, damn, James. That's perfect." Hank was vocal, all these little growls and rumbles coming from deep in his chest. James felt them vibrate against his lips, which was the best feeling.

He suddenly wanted a kiss—a real, full-on, tongue tasting

kiss that blew his mind and shared their flavors together. He lifted his face, begging for it, praying Hank was with him.

Hank gave him the kiss he craved without pause, taking his mouth by storm. That tongue pressed between his lips, Hank tasting him.

He groaned and pushed into Hank's arms, deepening the kiss, tongue sliding against Hank's.

They pressed together, Hank pulling James into his lap. Oh, so warm.

The hands on his ass burned him, all the way to the bone. He could feel that, for sure, so maybe he wasn't as broken as he'd feared. In fact, when his hips rolled, the action felt normal. Right.

"Mmmhmm." Hank slid one hand up under the back of his shirt. "God, yeah."

Yes. He needed skin on skin, needed their scents to mingle. He leaned so Hank could pull his shirt off too, and then they were rubbing, touching, sniffing. Yum.

He wanted to bite, but the kisses were too good, too heady, too right to ignore. They went on and on, slow and deep, then fast and hard enough to burn.

His body responded easily, his cock full and aching, his balls heavy. Oh. Oh, that felt so good. It wasn't magic or anything. He'd just been afraid to even try. Now he knew he was healing.

And just at the right time.

"Mmm...is this for me?" Hank's happy rumble felt almost as good as that hand on his flesh.

"Yeah." Hell, James felt pretty proud. He wanted to show it off.

"Excellent. I want it. Every inch." Hank had him out of his pants in seconds, hand rubbing and working his shaft. The feeling was so damn good he had to grit his teeth, his ass cheeks clenching. "Oh fuck. Look at you. You're perfect."

He tried to answer, but when Hank pressed one leg against his balls, he lost his words. His breath huffed out, and he moaned, his body on fire.

"That's it. Feel. I want to see you come."

James grunted, his need ratcheting up again, the heat searing him. He'd never burned so hot, so fast. Hank got to him. Period. He snapped his teeth at Hank's shoulder, and Hank let him bite, let him find a place to hang on.

He bucked and rolled, driving into Hank's hand, even as Hank groaned, whispering to him, making low, filthy promises. James wanted every one of them to come true, wanted every word to be reality.

"Tell me I can fuck you. Tell me I can feel your ass around my cock."

He nodded. He could catch and pitch. "Turn about's fair play. I want yours later."

"You know it." Hank paused. "I don't want to hurt you. Am I putting the cart before the horse?"

"I want you. I want to feel the good things." That was enough, wasn't it?

"Yes. That's perfect." Hank stroked him, up and down, the other hand creeping behind him, slipping between his cheeks.

The touch heated him, leaving him sweaty and aching, all the way to the bone, and he nodded, encouraging those fingers to continue.

"You're so damn hot. Oh, honey, I'm so glad I'm here with you."

"I dreamed about you. Over and over. You haunt me."

"I'm not sorry." Hank nibbled on his chin, then his neck. "I'm damn excited about it, in fact."

That hand squeezed tight, and he gasped, his head falling back.

"That's it, beauty. Feel me. We can do all sorts of things. Work up. We have time."

"I need to come for you. I ache." In the best way. He wanted to shoot.

"Well, come on then. I want to watch you, want to see your face." Hank stared into him, that hand never slowing down. The man had the freaking magic touch, driving him higher and higher.

Finally he had to lean into the touch and believe that he could allow the spring of need inside him to let go. It wasn't going to break him or make him explode.

Hank licked his lips, the sight so erotic it sent James over the edge. What a silly little thing to make him shoot like he was a teenager on his first date.

Hank watched him like he was amazing, though, like there was nothing funny about his need at all.

Thank God for that. If Hank had laughed at him and his O face, he might have scurried away forever and hidden in his office.

"Damn, baby. Damn. Look at you. And you smell like all the best sins. I should know."

"The best sins..." He would be more clever, but his brain was broken right down the middle.

"Mmmhmm. Like smoke and whiskey. All deep and rich and musky."

"Feels so good," James groaned, sighing deep in his chest.

"That's what I want. I want you to feel good." Hank was smiling, just looking so damn proud that James had to laugh.

"Have you seen my bed?" He dared to ask. "It's big enough for two."

"Is it?" Hank made with the wide eyes. "I just so happen to have a hard on that was made for a big bed."

"Excellent. Now I just have to figure out how to get to my chair without being clumsy and come-covered."

"There's nothing off putting about a man I've made come. I'll help." Hank eased him back, then stood up to offer a hand.

He took the hand, and this time he let his legs hold him, finding them weak and shaky, but holding.

"There you go." Hank helped him to the chair. "Do you do therapy?"

"I haven't left the building." He was scared to leave, if he was honest.

"Well, that's something we can do online, baby." Hank got him rolled to the bed. "I wanted you to have the chair in case you need it later. Now, where were we?"

"We were about to admire your 'needing a big bed' cock."

"We were!" Hank skinned out of his pants in a blink of an eye. His cock was still more than half hard, and he gave it a few yanks, which brought it back up to full, well, glory. Look at that.

James moaned, right out loud, and he rolled forward, drawn to it. Hank sat on the bed, stroking himself a few more times, showing off, he thought. Enticing him.

"Bed. Bed, so I can taste that."

Hank leaned forward to help him out of the chair, lifting him to lay atop Hank on the bed. "Hey."

"Hey. I want you. In all sorts of ways."

"I like the sound of that." Hank rubbed up against him, leaving a damp trail on his skin, which was already pretty coated.

"I'm going to suck you. I want to know your taste."

Hank's eyes went dark, the pupils dilating. "How do you want me?"

"Can you fuck my mouth?" It seemed the easiest and hottest, all at once.

"Can I? Jesus, yes. On your back?" Hank helped to ease him over, swinging his legs up. "Do you want any pillows?"

"Just one, yeah." It made for the perfect angle.

That flush told him Hank wasn't near as calm as he seemed, and while he was gentle with the pillow, he wasn't slow.

"Perfect. I need it now. Please." James grabbed Hank's hips and dragged that heavy, solid body up.

"Mmm. Me too." Hank rubbed against his lips with the head, slapping a little.

He opened up, tongue sliding out to taste. Oh, hot and salty. Addiction. He could get used to this.

He leaned up, lips wrapping around Hank's cockhead, tugging a little to tease. He wanted to test Hank's width, feel how he was shaped.

James loved the thick ridge around the flared head, the way Hank whimpered when he flicked the slit. Hank began to rock, hips moving slow and sure to start. He cupped Hank's ass, drawing him in close, filling his mouth.

That thick shaft spread his lips, making it hard to breathe a moment. Then he relaxed, pulling in air.

Together they found a rhythm, in and out—he sucked in as Hank pulled out. He let his lips drag all the way, giving friction, and Hank was vocal, telling him what a pretty mouth he had.

He blushed, because the praise made him shiver, made his spent prick jerk.

"So good, beauty. That mouth. Lick it, yeah. Suck it." Hank's hand sank into his hair.

He grabbed Hank's ass and pulled that sweet body closer, closing his lips around the tip and sucking hard.

He fucked the slit with his tongue, groaned as drops of salt spilled into him. Hank swelled even more between his lips, which was damn impressive. Then those hips really moved, Hank starting to fuck his face, just as promised.

That body made him sweat, made him pant, but he was just stirring. No round two for him, he thought.

He focused on giving Hank pleasure, answering all the sensation Hank had given him. He reached up, fingers lightly tracing the heavy, furry balls.

Hank yowled, the sound shocking and wonderful as it echoed through the room.

James wanted more of that. He wanted to feel and taste it when Hank came. He was starting to want all sorts of things.

He swallowed hard on every thrust in, sucking firmly so Hank had to fight to pull out.

"Fuck. Oh, God. James. So much. Gonna."

He loved that, the way Hank talked, gave it up for him. He nodded, taking Hank in to the root.

"Damn. Oh, damn. James." That and a tug to his hair was all the warning he got before Hank shot for him, filling him deep. He swallowed over and over, rolling Hank's balls and pushing gently to get every drop.

Hank hung over him for long moments, one arm braced on the headboard.

He hummed around the heavy cock, and Hank whimpered softly.

Maybe it was too much. Maybe Hank could go round two, though, even if he couldn't.

He looked up into Hank's eyes, the heavy-lidded pleasure.

"Damn, angel." Hank finally pulled free, then dropped to the bed next to him. "Damn."

He slid closer, snuggling up. "Hey."

"You're amazing." Hank kissed him, not one bit worried about where his mouth had been. He groaned and cuddled in, tongue sliding against Hank's.

"Mmmm." They just kissed and snuggled for the longest time. Somehow he thought life was never like books, but this was kinda.

It was warm, easy, and it made his hunger a little buzz along his nerves. The way it backed down and let him cuddle was a lovely thing; it wouldn't take much to stir it back up anytime.

"I like this. You've got a mouth made for sucking."

James felt the flush of pleasure on his cheeks. "Thanks. I think?"

That chuckle slid right along his spine. "Definitely a good thing."

"It was. You let me know when you want it again."

"Mmm. I will." Hank nibbled his jaw, and lights sparked all along his skin. He lifted his chin, purring deep in his chest. That was— had he ever had an afterglow? James didn't think so, and it made him want to be fuzzy in the best way.

"Come on. You can let him out, let me see."

"Yeah?" Shifting was so weird right now, but he really wanted to for the first time in ages, so James let it come.

"Yeah, there you are." Hank's fingers dug into his muscles, massaging him.

He moaned, his tail curling. So good. No one touched him when he was shifted, except to cuddle. This was different. This was sexual, sensual, and more than a little wonderful.

Not something he would ever try with Mick or Brock.

"So pretty, I love how long and fluffy you are."

He purred, letting his tongue drag on Hank's arm, pushing hard so his lover could feel it.

"Rough. Do I get to groom you? If I shift?"

He rowled softly. *Of course, pretty cat.*

Hank raised his eyebrows, but the shift came lightning fast, the bobcat right there.

So fuzzy. Such gorgeous feet. He rumbled softly, so happy.

There was no one else here now, and they could lick ears and whiskers, chew a little. Groom and play and roll together.

Hank batted at him gently, no claws involved. He twisted and turned, enjoying the touches. The sounds Hank made also really sent him over the moon.

He nuzzled into Hank's pretty belly, groaning deep in his chest. The scent there was so much stronger, and he rubbed his cheeks against the fur. Their scents mingled until he couldn't figure out which end was up, and that was okay. He didn't mind one bit.

This was like nothing else ever. This was amazing.

He'd never felt so calm, so heavy and relaxed.

Hank snuggled to him, weighing him down. They rolled to the center of the bed, Hank loving him into a doze.

His tail lashed as he melted down into the quiet of sleep.

FOUR

ank woke up naked and a little stiff, and not in the good way. His head was hanging off the bed, so he must have been all kitty when he went to sleep...

He heard a moan, a long, lazy yawn.

Oh, hello. He rolled his head up to look and there was James.

Mmm... his golden angel. He loved that, the relaxation, the peace in the smile James wore in his sleep. His... Man, that had happened fast, but he was damn possessive. James felt like his.

He admired the long lines, the body made for hunting and sleeping. That was something James needed that he'd been denying himself—long, lazy naps.

He'd been working too hard. Kit said James was obsessed, and he believed it. Of course, the other guys all said James had been the last one to move in, stubbornly maintaining his own place, and now he couldn't do that.

I'll protect you, golden boy. Angel. The thought was fierce, wild, and heady.

James curled over on one side, reaching for him. He took

James' hand, stroking the warm skin, loving the way he relaxed at his touch.

James' legs moved in his sleep, demanding exercise and work. They needed to get James walking. He'd start with a few YouTube videos on chair exercises, but James would be up and around in no time. Hank thought he was mostly scared. He couldn't imagine his brain telling his legs to move and it not working.

They healed fast, but James had been almost dead. That was tough to come back from. He stroked up James' arm, sending whatever healing thoughts he could. Lord knew he wasn't magical. James moaned, hips rolling like he was being fucked.

It was the most sensual movement he'd ever seen.

"Mmm. You're so hot, angel. I swear."

"Need..." James slid closer with a dreamy moan.

"Yeah? I'm right here. You're not just dreaming." Thank God.

"Good. Want you again." James pushed close and kissed him hard.

He hummed, kissing James, his body going from happy interest to need in a heartbeat.

James draped one leg over his hip, the motion natural and smooth as hell.

He pulled James up closer, dragging their skin together. Hot, fuzzy, James was a wet dream. His hand found James' ass, fingers curling in to pet.

James moaned, rubbing, clearly feeling that well. He'd just needed to believe, to have some stimulation. Hank dug his fingers in, waking those nerves, massaging the muscles.

"Oh." James stretched. "That feels so good."

"Looks good too." He could watch it forever.

"Yeah?" James opened his eyes, smiling. "Ditto."

"Mmm. I would flex, but I'm busy." Touching.

"You are. You're making me ache."

"I want to." Hank wanted everything with James. All of it. God he was an addict. Always had been. He'd never been addicted to a man like this though. Never. Coffee? The occasional cigarette binge? Food? Yeah. But not a person.

Moving his hands in slow circles, he kept rubbing, kept James groaning and writhing. He wanted to hear his mountain lion purr. Constantly.

"So pretty." Hank pinched one hip, watching to see if James jumped. The reflex test was instinctive on his part, but he knew it after the fact.

James jerked, rolling close to him.

Look at that. Feel it. James' cock rose hard and hot and wet-tipped against his hip. Yeah.

"Is this for me?" Hank asked.

James cupped his balls, offering himself over.

"Mmm. Oh, baby. That's it. I could eat you up." He nipped at James' neck, his hunger for this man growing with every second.

James purred deep in his chest, eyes rolling as he explored and nibbled, dragging his tongue on James' skin. That sound sent shivers down his spine, making him want to growl and pounce. He stayed gentle, though. For now. Roughhousing could come when James was a bit more confident in his body.

He knew it would come. He could see it now, and he just had to be patient.

Hank was an undercover cop slash agent. Patience could be his strong suit if it was worth it. James was so worth it. Stroking around to that flat belly, he grabbed James' cock, sliding his hand up and down.

"Oh." James sat up halfway before sinking back into the sheets.

"Uh-huh. It's irresistible. I just want to touch. So thick, angel. Beautiful."

He loved that blush, that rush of pleasure that he swore he could feel everywhere. Even deep in his mind.

That was probably just a reflection. Pleasing James made him so happy.

He began to stroke, up and down, making James' eyes cross. That was so cute, that expression, because the pink tip of that sweet tongue appeared too, James licking his lips.

His cock jerked, dancing at the thought of James' mouth.

"It was right, you fucking my lips. It made me ache."

He blinked down at James. "I want to return the favor. I want to fuck your ass too. I want it all."

"I'm in. Let's play."

He groaned and took a good, hard kiss. He wanted to turn this beautiful man inside out. James gave and gave and Hank had never had a lover so generous.

James' hand wrapped around the back of his head, fingers digging into his hair as they devoured each other. The kiss liked to burn his lips, it went so deep and hard.

He let his nails drag down over James, hard enough to sting, not enough to hurt.

Gasping, James bucked, those hips getting a hell of a workout. Poor baby would be sore, but it would be worth it. It was good for James, and Hank could offer to massage them later. He liked touching even when it wasn't super sexy times. Right now was definitely sex, though. Possibly even super sexy times.

"You're smiling." James stroked his cheek.

"Am I?" He was tickled, possibly over the moon.

"Yeah. That's good?"

"Hell, yes, angel. You make me smile." Hank kissed James' palm.

"Good. Good, I like to be..." James grinned sheepishly and shrugged like he didn't have the words.

"Mmm." He stroked some more, since he'd almost forgotten he was holding that cock.

"Oh." James blinked, pink tongue flicking out to wet those pretty lips.

He licked them, too, tasting James there. So sweet.

Heat suffused him, seeming to come from nowhere. God. Hank wiggled, just turned on and a little wigged out at how his pleasure seemed to keep doubling, tripling. He felt like he was flying, soaring through the air.

Lord knew, Hank had never left the ground before. Not during sex. This was something else. Maybe he was just doing it with the right kitty.

That was definitely the best possibility.

James kissed him again, then again, all but climbing into his lap. "Hey. Where'd you go?"

"I was thinking about you. I guess I was thinking not feeling, huh?"

"Thinking is fine. Feeling is better." James' touch to his balls was featherlight.

Hank's toes curled. "It is a fine thing when I'm with you."

James hummed in response, but those fingers kept petting and teasing.

His balls pulled up some, the hair rising on the back of his neck. "Damn, honey."

"You like that." James nuzzled his breastbone, soft hair teasing his nipple.

"Hell, yes. What kind of idiot wouldn't?" He stroked that hair, the thickness amazing. James seemed to be healing before his eyes. His body craved movement, not sitting all day.

He would so be the reason that James was well-exercised. No problem at all.

Hank bit a little, worrying James' lower lip, earning himself a low groan, and James' fingers trembled against his sac.

"Mmm. Now who likes that. You like a little rough sensation, huh?"

James shot him a quick glance. "I don't mind playing."

"Me either." Not one bit. Whoo.

"Excellent." James pushed up into his arms, taking a kiss that made his eyes cross. They were so on the same page, which was rad. Otherwise it could get weird.

He'd had a lot of weird lately. A lot.

This was meant to be a damn good thing. Something just his.

James straddled him, looking surprised at the ease at which he moved.

"That's it, baby. Hey. Look at you."

"I don't want to believe it, in case it goes away."

"Okay." He stroked that tight ass, the perfect globes shaping to his hands. "I'll believe for you."

"Fair enough." James kissed him again, good and hard.

They rocked together, and he wondered where he could get something slick. He could use spit, but he would bet it had been awhile, and James needed a little care.

"Here. In the headboard. There's a hidden drawer."

"Oh, sneaky. I like it." Digging inside he found lube and a little pack of tissues. It pleased him ridiculously that James used this lube for jacking off, maybe not liaisons. Except maybe with him.

"I'm a private cat, you know?"

"I know." He stroked that long back. "I'm glad you're letting me in."

James arched, moving long and slow, sliding against him. That sinuous movement made his mouth dry, so he licked his lips, then grabbed the lube so he could start to get James ready.

At the touch of his finger, James hummed, the soft rowl echoing inside him.

"That's sweet, baby. Sweet." He circled that hole.

"In me. I want you." *Now.*

"Just let me get you ready, love." No hurting. Not unintentionally.

A little slap and tickle, on the other hand...

James laughed the sound pure joy. "Not going to hurt me. I'm not fragile, lover."

Oh, didn't that sound good, that happy laugh? He wanted more of those noises. Well, and sex noises too.

James pushed right in, tongue sliding between his lips, fucking them nice and easy. Hank pressed one finger inside James' body, that tight hole clinging. He groaned and rubbed, stroking inside his cat until James gasped.

"That's it. Look how you're moving for me. Oh, baby, so good. I want to see you like this every day."

"Work-works for me. Fuck, Hank. Right there."

"Right here?" He hit that spot again, curling his finger just slightly.

The yowl that split the air made him grin. Everyone would know his mountain lion was getting off.

That suited him. Hank was doing this. Him. Making James feel amazing. He kept rubbing and tapping, intent on sending his cat over the moon.

"Tease. Fuck me."

"Not yet, baby. Not yet. I can make it even better."

"Yeah?" James didn't seem stressed out about it.

"Uh-huh. Just roll with it. Trust me." He smiled. Knowing James did trust him or he wouldn't be here.

"I'm good at rolling." James winked at him. "Don't stop."

"Not going to." Not until they both got what they wanted. He pushed and pressed, then pulled back to slip another finger in.

"Oh..." James' head fell back, throat working hard enough that his Adam's apple bobbed.

"Uh-huh. Look at you." Golden and lanky, lean where he

was stocky—James was perfect. Hank wanted to lick him all over.

"Not this time. Next time," James said. "This time you're gonna fuck me."

"Yes. Fuck yes. Need." He flipped James to his front, leaving that tight ass high in the air. He stroked down James' back with his free hand, wanting to relax James again, even as he pushed into that tiny hole.

He had the best view as the tiny ring of muscles spread and stretched around his fingers. Hank moaned. "Baby. You have no idea what you're doing to me."

"I'm needing you." *Craving you.*

Same here. Oh, honey. He just had to get in there with his dick.

Now. Now is good for me. James spread wide for him and let his hips cant up and back.

Hank slicked himself right up, praying they were doing the right thing. James wasn't in any pain, wasn't having difficulty moving, so he gave them what they both wanted, sliding home. His balls swung against James', his hips cradled against James' ass.

"More." James gripped the sheets, his body a long arc of pleasure. "More, honey. Please."

Hank had a ton more to give, so he moved his hips, rocking back and forth. It wasn't intended to be a tease, but he wanted to make his lion howl. They would rock and roll, then really get down to brass tacks.

He tilted James farther and drove down hard, dragging his cock against James' gland.

"Fuck!" James damn near growled it out, the word guttural. That tight hole clamped down on his cock until he grunted, gritting his teeth.

"Yes." He snarled back, loving the sound as their bodies slapped together.

Hank wanted to just go on like this for hours, but the pressure in his balls told him all good things would have to end sometime. Not yet, though. First he would reach under James and grab that bobbing cock so he could stroke it. The shaft was heavy and slick with pre-come, and the tip dripped with need. The scent of James' desire almost shoved him over the edge.

"God, baby." He snapped his teeth at James' shoulder, grazing that skin. "Making me crazy. Never been this close so fast."

The little bite made ass clamp down on him viciously.

"Oh!" He roared it, his body bucking, and then there was no more slow, no more easy. He was thrusting deep, sawing back and forth, their skin meeting with obscene noises. James met every thrust, every slap, every single growl.

That was the hottest damn thing he could ever remember happening to him in his whole life. This man wanted him enough to put aside fear and potential pain and take every single thing he had to give. He'd be damn honored, after he was finished coming so hard that he couldn't see.

That was close. So close he could feel the feathery edge of his orgasm going up and down his spine. He slapped his hand against the shaft of that heavy cock. "Now, baby. Now."

James screamed, the sound huge and wild, echoing as he shot.

That brought Hank right along with him, every nerve ending in his body firing as he came, his shout ringing in his ears.

They'd be lucky if Mick didn't break the door down to make sure they were okay.

If he does, I'll bite him.

"No biting the wolf. You want to bite, you come to me."

"And if I need you to bite me?"

"All you have to do is ask." He was still buried deep in

James. He could feel what that idea did to the man. This was the most fun he'd ever had. Ever. He kissed James' neck. "You might need to feed me."

"Steak? Burger? Sausages?"

"A burger could be good. You have any preference?" Hank wanted to know all the things James liked.

"I'll have Kit make bacon cheeseburgers with tater tots. He's the best cook."

"Yum. If it's okay with him, then yeah."

James snorted. "He loves to cook for people. Sometimes I think it's his true job, taking care."

"That would be a neat thing huh?"

"It is. Mick's good to him."

"So, are they a thing?" Kit sure looked at Mick.

"Not that I know of. I think Kit's waiting for Mick to see him."

"That sucks, man." A man could die inside waiting for someone to love him.

"Yes. God yes, but what are you going to do?"

"Well, me? Nothing." Hank winked. "Mick will figure it out, or Kit will move on."

"True that. We don't have to stress that part." James gave him the naughtiest grin.

"Nope. No stress. Just this. And food."

"Hand me my phone? Can you reach it?"

"Yeah." He stretched out and turned James to face him, which made them both moan, and James arched up, mouth unerringly finding his nipple.

"Uhn. Bad kitty." He laughed as they tangled up some.

"Super good kitty. Amazing." James nipped him hard.

"Gorgeous. Perfect. Precocious." He winked, then pinched that ass. The little yowl made him grin. "Food, perfect kitty. Food."

"Right!" James called Kit. "Hey, bear. What are you up to?

Yeah? We were craving burgers and tots…" James' eyes lit up. "Can you? You rock. Thank you. Thank you so much."

Hank chuckled. "Thank him for me too."

"Hank says thank you too, sweetheart." James winked at him. "No, we can come down. Yeah. Okay. Love you too. Bye."

"Lonely, is he?"

"Yeah. Brock and Griz are leaving a hole in the team."

"Griz is a wild man and one hell of a cop. I can't believe he settled down."

"Well, he and Brock had history." James shrugged. "I guess we need to clean up, huh?"

"Together?" Hank tried to go for casual.

"You help me in the shower?"

"Uh-huh." Score! Yeah, he totally would help. He knew if he could get James moving, in trusting his legs and getting stronger, he'd be fine.

"Thanks." James grinned, moving off him. "I can try, you know, walking behind the chair."

"I'll be with you every inch of the way."

"Thanks." James hid his nerves, but only barely.

"No worries, baby. You get tired, you sit."

"Right. And no one has to know but us, 'til I get it right."

"Exactly." He gave a quick kiss, proud that James was so willing.

James trembled as he stood, but he held himself up, taking shaky steps, one after another. By the time they hit the shower, James needed that teak shower seat, his legs quaking visibly, but he'd done so well.

Hank bent for a kiss, putting his pride, his joy in the caress.

James stroked his neck. "Thanks. That was… well, it was hard, but successful."

"It was. You'll have this."

James nodded, his expression pleased as hell.

"So, rub a dub?" Hank got the water going nice and warm. He could spend a little time on massage under the hot water.

"Sounds bubbly and fun." James watched him like a hawk, but the lean body was relaxed.

"It so does. Oh look, body wash." He got a really good lather worked up, then knelt down to start at James' feet.

"I—" James blinked at him, nice and slow. "You're spoiling me."

"I like that." He met James' eyes. "It feels a little selfish. Supposedly I help people all the time, but I feel like a total sleaze. Making you feel good makes me happy."

"You make me feel like a million bucks. Honest. No one's ever touched me like you."

"Good." He rubbed one instep. "I want you to feel good with me. I mean, all the time, but especially with me."

James dipped his head. "I hear you. I want to make you wild for me."

"I am, baby. Trust me." Now he dug into James' calves, rubbing hard.

"Oh!" James' eyes went wide. "Damn. I feel that everywhere."

"Yeah, those muscles have been working hard. I'm damn pleased."

"I am too. I—I am too."

"I think the guys will be ecstatic too." He really worked those legs, knowing it would help everything respond. He'd been shot once where it shattered his pelvis. It had taken longer than he approved of to heal.

Hank thought a lot of James' problem was fear.

That was why he was obsessed with the case. Had to be. If he solved it, he was safe again.

Hank leaned in and kissed the inside of James' thigh, loving to see the jump, the way James stared down at him.

"Did you feel that too?" James whispered.

"Yeah. I did. It's so cool, baby."

"I think it's you. I think you're helping."

"I hope so. I think you needed to get moving, but I'm all over helping and making it better."

"I needed a hand. Someone...from a dream?" Oh, look at that blush.

"You did. I'm glad you found me." He rubbed James' thighs next, and James opened up like he'd pressed a button.

"Mmm. Now, remember, we only have so much time." He soaped James up, then stroked him to rinse off.

"Uh-huh. I'm not asking. I swear."

"I know, baby. It just feels so good." He leaned in, kissing James' chest.

"And I feel like I'm burning for you."

"I know. I just want to keep touching you."

James nodded and drew him in for another kiss. "After food, I think we can take an afternoon to... explore."

"I think that's a fine idea. A really fine." James was proving to be a sensual, eager lover, and it was a little like watching someone come to life.

He sighed, then soaped up the rest of their bodies. He really was hungry, and he thought Kit was lonely as hell, so they needed to get on.

"We will do that then. Kit and Rey are best Dr. Who friends so they can live without us, don't worry."

"Yeah? I never was a sci-fi fan..." He liked noir and hard case mysteries.

"Kit is addicted. It's cute. I'm a horror fan, myself. It makes me smile."

"I like horror. Especially movies." Hank rinsed them, then got up to turn off the water.

James tried to push himself up to standing, but those

poor, overworked legs were like noodles, and Hank had zero intention of letting his lover fall.

So they danced out to the chair, Hank drying James off some before easing him down. "Clothes, huh?"

"At least sweats and socks. We're not formal at all."

"Can I borrow some?" He hated putting dirty clothes back on.

"Of course. I have lots." Together they managed clothes, and then they headed down to the communal area, finding everyone together—Mick and Dylan playing cards, Kit and Rey playing a video game.

"Hey." James rolled into the room, and everyone stopped to look at them, a few eyebrows going up.

"Hey, man," Dylan said.

"Hey!" Kit bounded over to hug them both. "Okay, let me finish up lunch."

"Do you need any help?" James rolled right over.

"Yeah. If you want to get the garden ready, that would be great." Kit looked so tickled.

"Come and sit, Hank. The guys have it." Mick nodded to one of the chairs.

"What are you playing?" he asked, sliding into the seat.

"Cribbage. Wanna play?"

"Deal me in." He could slay at this game. Math was a good thing for him.

Mick moved the score pegs back to start and dealt. "How's it going?"

"Good." He glanced at James. "I mean, I'm not sure we're making a lot of progress on the case."

Mick snorted. "I'm not sure it is a case."

Dylan raised an eyebrow. "You don't believe in coincidence, boss."

"And I believe in conspiracies. But this is... It may be until we're supposed to know, we won't know." Mick shrugged and shook his head. "I don't care. James has been downstairs twice in two days. You're hired."

"Uh." He blinked. "What do you mean? Really? You would give me a job." His stomach flipped right over, he would swear. Surely Mick was joking.

"I will. Am. Yes." Mick didn't seem stressed in the least.

"Oh." Hank had a new job. He did. His heart was pounding.

Dylan caught his eye. "You want to do undercover shit the rest of your life?"

"God no." Hank took a deep breath. "I need to talk to James. And my handler."

"Fair enough. We want you here. Brock and Griz say you're solid. You let me know."

"Thanks." Jesus. His world had just turned on a dime. He was burned out, but he would never step on James' toes.

James rolled over to them, searching his face with those pretty gold-green eyes. "You okay?"

"I am. Fixing to clean up here."

"Yeah, excellent." James shot him a happy little grin. "Food is coming up fast. Look alive."

"You got it." He grinned, his whole body on high alert. This could be his. Damn.

Damn.

His mouth watered when Kit brought over a platter of burgers and tots. "These have cheese. These don't."

"Thanks, kiddo," Mick said. "Smells amazing."

"It really does. I'll do dishes." The little fox bounced up, landing in Dylan's lap.

"Cool." Kit winked. "I bet Dylan helps."

"Not much of a cook, fine dishwasher."

"Can you cook, Hank?"

Hank grinned. "I can. Kinda specifically."

Kit tilted his head. "What does that mean, exactly?"

"It means my best friend in high school was Italian. Like whoa. His mom taught us both to cook so when we went away to college, we wouldn't starve. You want gnocchi? I'm your man."

Kit moaned, eyes rolling back in his head. "Tomorrow? I'll help."

"You bet, buddy. I can make all kinds of sauces too. Pesto. Alfredo. Sunday gravy." Hank winked. His only skill.

"Oh, Mick. Can he stay?"

"Up to him, huh?" Mick gave them all a wide grin. "I made the offer."

Hank glanced at James, trying to gauge what he thought of that.

James looked up at him, meeting his eyes. *Are you staying?*

Wait. Had he— Was that?

I would like to. He thought it like a bit of a prayer. He really did want to see where this could go.

James' eyes lit up, and he got a nod, a grin. James had heard him.

Oh, fuck him raw. Yeah, his life was about to change hugely, because there was no way he was letting go of this. No way.

"Dude, are you okay?" Dylan grabbed his arm and eased him down into a chair.

"Huh? Yeah." When had he stood up? Hank chuckled. "Sorry. Burger."

"Cheese?"

"Yeah, thanks."

James glanced at Hank, worried, but he didn't say anything, just took his plate from Kit with a smile. "Thanks, honey. It smells great."

I'm giddy. I'll call my boss tomorrow. He felt like everything was new and laid out in front of him like the Yellow Brick road.

Yeah? He loved that smile on James' face.

Uh-huh. I just got a little ahead of myself. Kinda like something had grabbed him and pulled him up.

Relief can do that. Relief and shock.

Yeah. I—I have a lot of feels, baby. Hank grabbed a burger and added mayo, mustard and pickles.

James was a tomato, lettuce, and mustard guy—good to know.

In fact, Hank paid attention to what all the guys liked so he could buy sometime soon.

Kit was an omnivore, where Mick was a meat, cheese, bacon, bread and mayo type. Dylan and Rey just wanted ketchup and onions.

His first paycheck would totally go to burgers.

He glanced at Mick, who raised an eyebrow. "I do business meetings first thing. We'll talk salary and bennies tomorrow at nine."

"I'll call my handler tonight. I'll need to get my clothes at some point soon." Lists started forming in his brain, but he would have to write them all down.

"Sure. Someone will go with you."

"Not Dylan." Hank shrugged. "He looks too much like a cop."

"I'll go with," Kit offered. "I'm good at carrying boxes."

"Thanks, hon. I don't have much where I'm staying. Later I'll need to get some stuff out of storage, but after anyone stops looking for me." His handler might set up an accident for him or something.

"No problem. A guy needs his clothes and DVDs."

"Yeah." His only electronics were his phone and said DVDs, which worked better than streaming for a guy who couldn't leave a trail. "Man, it will be nice to level up to a place like this."

"You already have an apartment, so it works perfectly." Rey grinned at him. "Welcome aboard!"

"Thanks, foxy." He winked when Rey clapped his hands and laughed.

"You're welcome." Rey bowed dramatically, right from Dylan's lap.

James hooted, looking so happy. Hank wanted to keep that expression there. In fact, he'd do a lot for that simple joy, the pleasure that came from him staying.

He wanted James more than he'd ever wanted anything. Ever.

The rush of warmth and wonder that slid along his nerves was pure magic.

Hank couldn't stop smiling. Giddy. This was what giddy felt like.

They all ate, jabbering the entire time about nothing at all, and it was like having a family again, having a spot.

How long had it been? Undercover just isolated a man.

James reached out, one hand solid and hot on his thigh, steadying him there.

Hank took a deep breath, then let it out. Yeah. He just needed to breathe. In and out. In and out.

"The burgers are good, aren't they?"

"They're..." He took a bite. "Yummy."

"Mmhmm..." Was James purring?

Hank licked his lips. God, James was something. Hot as fire.

The purring got louder, settling right in his balls. All he could do was nibble his food and stare. At James.

Every time he blinked over, James was watching him, eyes on his mouth. Hank licked his fingers, showing off a bit.

I could suck that...

You could. His cheeks heated.

"Stop it, you two." Mick winked to take the sting out of the growl.

"What?" James went for innocent, and it so didn't work.

"Uh-huh."

"Eating." James had a tot, then smacked his lips.

Mick didn't look mad. He looked pleased as punch.

"Nom?" Kit teased.

"Hell yes." Dylan groaned, patting Rey's belly, which was the cutest thing ever.

James chuckled softly, hand beginning to stroke his thigh.

He tensed all up, but it was all good.

This okay?

So good. Getting me all hot.

I like to hear that. James' gorgeous green eyes held his.

Me too. You make me crazy in a happy way. He touched James' hand.

"You two need some alone time." Mick's voice was soft, rumbling.

"We do. Sorry, guys. Kit, thank you."

"Take a plate with you for later," Kit said. "You'll need it."

"Listen to you." James blushed dark, but Hank? He just grabbed some burgers. He thought that sounded like a great idea. Never pass up sustenance.

"If you'll hold the food, I'll push you," he offered, feeling a little daring.

"Run." James laughed, taking the plate.

"I can do that. Afternoon, guys. I'll see you tomorrow, Mick."

"Good deal." Mick waved them off.

"You won't get in trouble?" Hank asked.

"He's been trying to get me to rest." James grinned up at him. "I want to be with you."

"I want that too, baby." It was like a compulsion, but

Hank wasn't one to question fate. They had this new bond to explore.

"New relationship energy, huh?"

No. No, he didn't think it was exactly that. He thought it went deeper. Bigger. He thought this was a forever thing.

James glanced over one shoulder at him, pupils dilating. Yeah. That was something else, that thought. He swooped down and took the kiss he needed, forcing himself to keep things as light as he could.

They were still in the hallway, after all.

"Upstairs, Hank." He loved this—commanding James.

"Mmmhmm. More." The elevator took forever. Soon they would be able to shift and race up the stairs. Right now he wanted to strip down and touch, groom each other, touch whiskers and spread their scent until the bed smelled like both of them.

Then he wanted to do naughty things as men. Very naughty.

Possibly filthy. He felt like James would be there, right with him.

The touch to his ass said he was right. Hoo yeah.

Time for a little fun with his own personal lion.

FIVE

James pulled himself to standing, forcing himself to walk to the bathroom, each step exhausting. Hank was right; he could do this. Mostly. His feet wanted to stumble, and his legs shook, but damn. Damn, it felt good. He was going to surprise them all when he finally walked into his office.

He grinned, then cursed when he tripped, going crashing into the door jamb.

"Baby? You okay?" Hank's sleepy voice was adorable.

"Uh-huh." He was just going to stay right here a second and breathe.

"You holler if you need help." He loved that Hank was letting him do it himself, but he wasn't sure he—

No, he could.

He had to. Leaning here forever was going to become uncomfortable.

He chuckled. Okay. Move. Come on, buddy, before you fall.

He pushed himself up and focused on holding himself up, taking one unsteady step after another. He did his business, then headed back, and he got to the bed before his legs gave out or before he burst into tears because damn, he was worn.

"Hey. Good job, baby." Hank's hands slid over his lower back.

"Thanks. Thank you." He panted softly, trying to keep himself from crying out.

"Shhh. There's no shame in it, baby. You worked hard, and now you're sore." Hank rubbed, which made him moan. "Stretch out here on the mattress so I can help."

James did as Hank asked, turning onto his belly.

"That's it."

His legs jerked, not really under his control, but the more Hank massaged, the better that got. Hank's fingers knew just where to touch him, how to love him. It wasn't about sex—not yet anyway. This was healing.

He groaned, his toes curling, then releasing. "Good."

"Mmhmm...pretty kitty." Hank groaned softly, the sound hungry.

He grinned, stretching out longer. "You're up and at 'em."

"You're inspiring." Hank cupped his ass and squeezed, just enough to let him feel it.

"So are you." His body reminded him how much he'd recovered already, his cock growing hard. He'd never needed so much, so desperately, and it was insane.

Hank made him... crazed with want. But it was more than that too. He felt like he knew Hank deep in his bones. He felt like this was—meant to be? Why else would he have dreamed about this man so much?

"I feel that way too, you know," Hank said. "I really do."

"Are you scared?" He'd never believed he could find his one, his other half, his mate.

"No, baby. I'm full of all sorts of sky-high feelings, but I'm not scared." Hank rolled him over, raising him up to kiss him.

He melted, jonesing on that confidence, the surety. He

missed Brock, the way he brought that attitude, making things feel safe.

The kiss took him flying, going deep and hungry. Hard. Necessary to the bone.

He sighed and stretched, long and slow. James loved the feel of Hank against him, wanted more of it in his life.

"Mate." He opened his eyes as he spoke the word, hoping that Hank heard him, accepted that.

"Yeah, baby. Yeah, I am." Hank licked his lower lip.

"Oh. Me too."

"Good." Hank licked him. Then kissed him again, and he wanted to scream his pleasure to the world. His legs wrapped around Hank, and he tried to hold on, clamp down even as shaky as the muscles felt.

"Mmmm. Getting stronger all the time." Hank sounded so proud.

"I'm trying. Hard." Getting strong, walking, figuring out how to recover.

"I know. I'm proud."

The words were simple, but god he needed to hear them. Nothing had felt right for so long, and now it was starting to again. He was beginning to feel—real.

"You are real, baby. So wonderful." Hank sort of wallowed on him, then bit his neck.

He lifted his chin with a soft yowl.

"Right there, huh?" Hank bit again.

"Yes." The zing that hit him left him growly and purring, all at once.

Hank hummed, the sound so satisfied, so damn happy. *Why wouldn't I be happy? I have my mate between my teeth.*

James chuffed, loving how Hank thought about things. That was tickling him to death.

"I can't believe I found you, but now that I have, you're all mine."

"Yes. Yes, I am." Hank licked the spot where he'd bitten.

He sucked in a sudden, hard breath, his eyes rolling back in his head.

That's even better, huh?

It's big, mate. I feel it everywhere.

I want you to. Hank worried the spot over and over. It seemed to get bigger, like that buzz and ache was going to take him over.

Just feel it, baby. There's nothing wrong with it.

"I could lose myself in you." Lose himself and be happy doing it.

"Good." Hank touched him everywhere, hands sliding on him, his pajamas melting away.

"Is it normal? To want you all the time? Is this reasonable?" Did he care?

"I think it is. I mean, we're mating, baby." Hank drew back to look into his eyes. "That only comes in wild for each other."

"Each other. Fuck, that's the best part. Each other."

"Yes. You and me." Hank squeezed his ass, making his muscles clench. It was like his man knew all his hot spots.

"Damn." He rolled his hips, meeting Hank's hands.

"Uh-huh. What do you want, baby? I could eat you alive."

"Okay. I'm all yours." He pinched one of Hank's nipples and rolled it between his fingers.

"Oh!" Hank jumped, then laughed out. "Do it again."

"I can manage that." This time he tugged, a little hard.

"Uhn!" Hank arched, his whole body bowing. "Baby. Yeah. Like that."

He bent to bite the other, switching back and forth, teasing and playing. This was the best thing ever, taking time to be with someone, touching and laughing and having amazing, mind-blowing sex...

No wonder Brock had asked for a few months off to

explore and play with his bear. Good thing it was slow right now.

James faltered a moment, wondering if he was endangering his team.

"I'll help you put pieces together tonight, baby. We'll work on it." Hank was reassuring, not humoring, which he appreciated.

"Thank you. I don't want them hurt. Any of them."

"No, I get that. You guys are tight. Amazing." Hank grinned. "Even if the cops think you guys are hopeless."

"Did they really say that?" James asked.

"A few guys have said it. I don't think they've ever encountered werecrocs or weasels with drug-poisons."

"Someone's crazy and wants to hurt us. It's like being old-school Batman or something."

"It is." Hank pulled him into a warm embrace, and while he mourned the loss of the mood they were having, it felt good to be heard. Seen. Mick tended to act like he was an obsessed kid about all this.

Then again, Mick was furious and worried. He tended to get a little dismissive and inward focused when he was worried for them. It was a thing.

"Who hates y'all enough to cause this much trouble?"

"I don't know. I mean, maybe Patel has reason now, but he didn't before. Just like the drug guy, Hetrick. He's got reason now, but why us before? I keep digging but two and two is coming up six."

"Then it's someone who isn't one hundred percent open with you." Hank chewed that lush lower lip. "I got to say, what about Brock?"

"What about him?" He fought his growl. "He's a good man, Hank. My soul brother. He wouldn't hurt us."

"No, I know that. I've worked with him. But he was black

ops. He has to have some enemies." Hank stroked his hip, soothing.

"Right. Right, I don't know. He doesn't talk about it. Not ever. Not to me. Maybe Mick knows?" James didn't think so, though. Not at all.

"Huh. Okay. Well, we might have to Skype him. That can't interrupt them too much, can it?"

"No, and if it does, too fucking bad. We need to fix this shit."

"Good man." Hand gave him a wink, then another hug. "See? We're golden."

"Yeah. Yeah. I—this is my home, my family, the first and only one I've had. I need it to be safe." James held Hank's gaze. He'd been a foster kid, in college before anyone, just a freak. Always.

"I can see that." Hank stared right back, serious as a heart attack. "I barely know everyone, but this pack is special. I can tell."

"Yeah. This is...we're home and I almost lost it." And that had scared the living shit out of him. The idea that this could simply disappear.

"We'll get this figured out." He thought that might be Hank's work voice. It sounded a lot like Dylan's cop voice.

It was surprisingly comforting. Hot.

He grinned. He was such a dork. At least Hank was aware of that fact, right?

"Totally, babe." Hank snorted. "Like I'm the epitome of cool or something. I like Mickey Spillane, and Deadpool and Food Network shows."

"I like *Ghost Hunters* and *Live Shifters.*"

"Well, there you go. As long as you'll watch baking shows with me, I'll watch paranormal shit with you."

"Fair enough. I have all the streaming. We can binge."

"I love that." Hank scratched his belly. "Mmm. I also like to snuggle. Did I tell you?"

"You're a feline like me. Napping, snuggling, and sunlight are necessary."

"They are. I know we're supposed to be all solitary, but we're human too."

"We're not meant to be alone forever. None of us. We need each other."

"Right?" Hank traced his belly. "I—I thank the universe every day that y'all found me, that I met you. Even when I thought I would never see you again."

"I dreamed about you, Hank. I couldn't stop. You were in my goddamn soul."

Hank nodded, reaching up to cup his cheek with one hand, his fingers gentle. "I hope to stay that way. God, baby." Hank kissed him again, and he thought maybe they'd found that mood again.

He thought they were going to find it again and again.

———

Hank watched James sleep for a bit, then he got up so he could grab his phone, which was a pretty powerful machine, and do a little research. He adored their time together, but at some point, he would have to work for his keep, and to do regular cases, they had to be able to leave the agency.

Right?

So, he knew James had looked into all of the bad guys, but had he really dug into his team members?

As far as he could tell, this either hinged on Brock or Dylan. Rey was new, an unknown...but he could see what James meant, the fox was dear. And pretty open. He might have brought in Patel by accident, but he wasn't the reason for the undercurrent of danger Hank sensed.

Dylan had been a cop a long while. He'd put away dozens of criminals, and some might have enough pull to do the kind of damage this one had.

Then again, Brock had even more enemies, he would bet. But how many had ever seen Brock's face?

Dylan. He needed to talk to Dylan—he'd been a cop, he got it, and he knew Rey.

Hank slipped on some clothes before heading to the office to see who was about. He felt a little illicit, but James needed the rest. His body was working hard to heal.

And Hank needed to talk to Dylan, cop to cop.

"Hey!" Dylan caught him on the way in, coming out of the common room with coffee and holding a doughnut. "How goes?"

He had to laugh about the doughnut. Had to. "Good. Good, I was coming to chat with you, honestly. Got a minute?"

"Sure. Want anything to bring with?" Dylan nodded back toward the coffee maker.

"You know, why not?" He could be a cliché too, no sweat.

"Cool. The doughnuts are good. Kit ordered them in from a new place."

"Totally non-ironically, right?"

"Totally."

"Cool." Hank grabbed a coffee and what looked like a maple bacon doughnut. Salty.

Hank followed Dylan to what must be the man's office, the room an utter disaster, boxes and papers everywhere, the desk nightmare. God, he felt at home.

They grinned at each other. Cops.

"So, what's up?" Dylan asked.

"Well, you know James is obsessed with finding a connection to what's going on."

"Some, yeah. Rey says it's a little scary."

"You should see his whiteboard." Hank winked. "The one thing he's reluctant to do is dig too deep into the team."

"You're talking about Brock." The surety in Dylan's voice made him blink.

"What do you know that I don't?" When Dylan gave him side-eye, he spread his hands. "I'm James' mate, man. You might as well know. I would never hurt you guys."

"No shit? Good on you. James doesn't know about Brock? They're close as brothers."

Hank snorted. "What all do you tell your friends that you don't tell your sibs?"

Dylan laughed. "Lots of shit. My people don't speak to me."

"There you go. He was in some heavy shit, huh?"

"Him and Locke both. You said you did some black ops, so you get it. They worked together. Brock was out in the wind longer, though, and he had some heavy shit happen back in Brazil, I think. The details are hazy."

"Can we dig them up without bringing it down on his, or our, head?"

"We can try." Dylan grinned. "That's what we do, right? I mean, James is all electronic. He can get flagged. We nibble in from the edges, make calls, send out feelers quietly."

"Yeah. I got a hunch that this is someone after Brock, someone who's trying to make him suffer through the team." Hank wasn't sure why he thought so, but he didn't stress it. He trusted his gut.

Dylan chewed his lower lip a moment. "You think that's why Brock and Griz left? Like he knows something?"

"I think they wanted to bond, but if he was worried, it's something he would do, right?" Hank asked.

"Yes. Absolutely. What if he's trying to draw fire from us?" Dylan met his eyes with a growing horror.

"Yeah. Then he and Locke—Griz—are pretty vulnerable."

"We have to go to Mick."

Such a wolf, always going to the alpha when something new came to light.

"And what will Mick want to do?" Hank asked, knowing the answer. Still, he wanted Dylan to think about it.

"Go get them…" Dylan sighed. "We need a few days to research."

"Exactly. If we find something we go to Mick."

"Fair enough, but if Mick asks, I can't lie."

"Also fair." They shook on it. "Okay, so where do we start, man? I can make some calls in my former department, but that will also throw flags. They're feds."

"There's a guy… Let me see what I can do. Cor's a decent son of a bitch, for a con man."

"Wow. I knew you were the go-guy." He bit into his doughnut. "Oh, that's good."

"Yeah. Yeah, they don't suck." Dylan shook his head. "I wonder what set this off…"

"You mean like there had to be an inciting incident…" Listen to his cop speak.

"Something had to cause it, and I know it wasn't my mate." Dylan's eyes shined bright for a moment.

"Okay, why not? I mean just help me rule it out." He wanted to hear it, even though his gut told him the same thing.

"Rey was an information broker—the wrong file fell into his hands and people died. He came to us scared, but that's all. He gave the data over. Patel was arrested."

"Right. Man, I need a notebook."

"Got one." Dylan pulled a little spiral work notebook out of his desk, handing it to him with a pen.

"Talk to me about Patel?" He hoped he'd hear something Dylan didn't know he was thinking.

"Uh, timeline-wise that was the start. He was the one who

had killed Rey's client. Tiger shifter with crocodile hench-men." Dylan growled. "They kidnapped Rey and practically demolished the office."

"That's horrifying and amazing. You're the only people I know that have come face to face with crocodile shifters." Hank made notes. "Where did you guys go?"

"Brock's safe house."

His head tilted. Whoa.

"That was when he called Locke in, too. To help when Rey was kidnapped."

Hank blinked. Okay. So, Brock's house was revealed, and an old friend/lover entered the scene...

"And he knew Locke from his black ops days?"

"Yeah. They were tight, I guess. Then Brock got involved with a bunch of stuff and Locke went to work on another team. I think?" Dylan got out his own notebook. "I'll fact check that."

"Yeah, because if the end game was getting to Brock—now he's separated from his entire team."

"Christ." Dylan's shoulders were like rocks. "It goes against everything, not telling Mick." He held up a hand. "I get it, but as soon as we know something..."

"Yes. The second we do, we blow the lid off—until then, this is between us."

Dylan nodded, lips pressed into a tight line. "I feel like we've all had blinders on. This shit has made me feel like an amateur."

"Well, it's time we all started acting like pros."

"It's hard when it's your family."

Hank nodded. "I'll be the fresh eyes, I promise." He would also do the hard work of telling the rest of the team if need be. This was a bitch, but he believed that no one on this team was directly responsible.

It was someone's past rearing up to meet them, he would bet. Someone damn grumpy, from the sounds of it.

"Well, we have a direction now." Dylan gave him a wry grin.

Hank? Are you— is everything okay?

His eyes crossed a little when he heard James' voice in his head. Hank still wasn't used to that.

"Weird, huh? It's like having a crazy emotional intercom."

I'm getting doughnuts. "It is. I'm a decent multi-tasker, but damn."

Oh...me too? Please? I'm heading for the shower.

I'm on my way up. "Okay, let's do some research and share what we find out? James wants a doughnut."

"He likes the apple fritters."

"Oh, good to know." He grinned. "What does Rey like?" They rose as one, heading for the office door.

"Blueberry cake." Dylan rolled his eyes. "But I forgive him."

"You're a giver, I'll let you have that."

"Right? Okay, man. We'll rendezvous tomorrow."

"On it." Hank slipped into the common room and grabbed three more doughnuts. Two of them were apple fritters. And coffee. Lalala.

He walked in to find James on the sofa, no wheelchair in sight. Look at that. All clean, too, and smelling of manly soap.

"Hey, baby. How you feeling?" He set the doughnuts and coffee down before sitting next to James and begging a kiss.

"Good. Good, I did it. I made it to the bathroom and out here."

"I see that. And you left the chair in the bedroom." Hank gave his lover a thumbs up. "That's exceptional."

"I may never move again. Ever." James winked up at him. "But I did it." And his mate was glowing with effort and pride.

"Apple fritters will help give you strength." He presented them with a flourish.

"Oh yum. Thank you." James pounced on them, chowing down. His mate was healing. He needed to get protein in James.

He made a note to ask Kit what other wonders James liked besides burgers and steaks. Maybe some crispy chicken or wings...

He'd bet his lion loved wings.

Man, Hank knew he'd gotten spoiled really fast with the food. These guys ate like kings...

"We have a large grocery budget, love."

"I bet. Boneless wings, or bone in?"

"Boneless." James grinned. "Kit buys them by the bag, then makes his own sauces."

"He's a treasure." He bent to take a soft kiss. "I'll order some in a bit."

"Cool. Spoiling me."

"You need protein," Hank said. "And I can't wait to find out all your favorites."

"Who told you about the fritters?" James asked.

"Dylan. He was getting coffee."

"Ah. Cop shop talk."

"You know it. I like him a lot." Dylan was a solid guy for a wolf.

"I love how he treats Rey. I do. He's always been a little growly, but he treats Rey like a king."

"He's a wolf. And a cop." Hank winked. "So, what should we do today?"

"Tiddlywinks? Movies? Blowjobs?"

"Damn. You go big." He winked. "I could go for all of those. I might have to, uh, work out. If I'm gonna eat this much."

"There's a gym downstairs." James winked broadly. "I could watch."

"You could. You could work out with me?"

"Yeah, if no one's down there..."

"Okay. We can take the chair, just in case." He knew James wanted to surprise everyone, but he could also use some cardio or strength training.

"Sure. I should get back to work too, shouldn't I?"

"Nah." He fed James another bite of doughnut. "We're not hurrying."

"No?" James snapped the bite up.

"Nope. Dylan says there's nothing new on, and you say Mick would call us in if we need to work, so boom." He licked his fingers.

"But the other?" James motioned to his wall.

"We can work on that for sure." He nodded, sobering so James knew he was there to help.

"Yeah. I want to find him so we can be safe again. All of us."

"I want that too." He would rip the person who had hurt James apart with his bare hands if he had to. "Whoever it is, they have to have a huge bank of resources to control men like the ones who have come after you."

"Yes. And we don't. Mick's not poor, but Apex needs clients, and we can't take on clients while we're in hiding."

"Okay, now that I can see." He winked, but it was a legit concern. A man had to be able to make money. Including him.

"Yeah."

He hated that worried line that popped up between eyes, so he reached up to smooth it out.

"Hey, we can do this. We're smart kitties, and everyone is on it. We have some direction now."

"Yeah. Yeah, direction is good, right?"

"Well, it's better than running in circles I guess." He laughed. "When in doubt, look at the next thing. Cop 101."

"When in doubt, dig deeper and look for the backdoor in." James winked at him. "Hacker 101."

Hank hooted. "We'll make a good team, baby."

James nodded seriously. "Rey and Dylan do. They're kinda like us, right?"

"You're eighty times hotter." He held gaze. "You make me stupid with need."

James sucked in a slow breath. "Yeah?"

"Yep. No doubt about it." Hank saw no reason to deny it. His mate.

James blushed dark, and he saw it, how James saw himself as pale and lean, plain. As if he wasn't the most beautiful man Hank had ever seen. Which he was. His golden lion, his green-eyed lover.

Hank tried to let James see him through his own eyes. He knew better than pale and beige.

His cat was sensual and bright, wickedly smart, fine and lithe. Everything Hank craved. He could explore this man the rest of his life and never get bored.

James pounced him, the motion quicker than he could see, teeth dull on his shoulder. "Mate."

Hank grunted, hands on James' hips, holding him close. "More."

Those bites were enough to make him howl, make him throw back his head and rowl like, well, a cat in heat. Jesus, he was hot as fire, and ready to explode in a heartbeat.

Mine. teeth traveled down his ribs, the sensation driving him crazy.

Yes. Yes, yours. God. James. Thank God for mental babble, because Hank had lost real words.

Mine. I dreamed about you. Dreamed about your cock, your laugh, your eyes. Everything.

I couldn't wait to get back to you. I was in limbo. Hank touched everything he could, all that bare skin, just waiting for him.

I was afraid I was alone.

Not anymore. I have you. That was something James could count on.

James looked up at him, eyes shimmering and bright, and he knew James *heard* him. God. He was— he didn't even know what he was. Excited and pleased as punch and hot as a sidewalk in July.

Then James took him in, lips dropping over his cock.

He roared like he was a big cat and not just a bobcat, his body bucking. He would never get tired of this, not in a million years. Not even in two.

James swallowed around him, over and over, pulling him hard and drawing him in. Hank sawed back and forth, grunting, his whole body alight. His mate had his ass, tugging at him, letting him fuck those pretty lips.

His belly pulled in, his chest heaved, and his balls went tight. So fast. James got to him so fast.

Gorgeous. James groaned around his cock, the sensation settling in the small of his back.

He petted James' hair, watching it curl around his fingers. "So hot." There. Words.

Warm hands nudged his balls, making him grunt. Yeah, hot.

He humped and moaned and tried to share what he was feeling with James. Was that possible? He hoped so. This was pure pleasure. He wanted to give that back, but he just couldn't make his body do anything but what it was doing at this moment.

Feel, mate. Just let go and feel me.

Yes. Okay, yeah. He could do that. He needed to be able to let loose more, and with James he was safe. He could fly.

He could fucking soar.

James groaned around him, head bobbing, giving him what he needed.

Hank was gonna blow any second, so he stroked James' shoulder, letting him know. James swallowed, making his eyes cross and he howled as he came, unable to hold back any longer.

Jesus, this might just kill him.

If it did, what a way to go.

He lay there, panting, until he felt James humping the couch. Then he grabbed the man and yanked him up for a kiss.

"Mate." James was all growls and grunts.

"Uh-huh." He got his hand around James' cock, stroking. "Just want you so bad."

"You have me. All the way."

He nodded, biting his lower lip as he worked James up and down. Hank wanted to see James come. He needed to see James lose himself.

So he flicked his thumb, letting it slap the tip of James' cock, knowing it would sting.

"Hank!" James arched and cried out, so hungry, so full of need.

"Come for me, lover. Come on. I want to feel you in my hand."

"Any-anything." James began to hump him, hard and steady, driving against his palm.

"That's it." He moved his thumb again, just so, letting James really experience the sensation. He could feel the white-hot need, the wild hunger, pouring over him, letting him share in pleasure.

Then James was coming for him, adding molten seed to the mix.

James slumped down and cuddled in, moaning for him.

"Damn, baby." What else could he say? It never got any less exciting, and he couldn't see it ever being that way.

"Uh-huh. No shit on that."

"Have I said thank you for letting me come be with you?" That gratitude filled his belly and chest, burning away the sad emptiness of his undercover adult life.

"I needed my mate. You. I needed to know you."

"I get that." He pulled James down into a more comfy position. "I know now."

"Me too." James got heavy, his lover finally beginning to rest.

He wanted James to sleep some more. To just really let his body get healed.

Hank felt fiercely protective. He hadn't had much in his life, but this man, this lion was his and his alone.

Hank would share with the team; they were family, but he wouldn't give James up now. Not for anything. For the first time, he had something of his own.

He kissed James' jaw, letting them settle in for, well, a cat nap.

Maybe he had a little recovering to do of his own.

Six

"Tell me about why you came to Apex, Rey?" James thought they should start where the trouble had, and that was when Rey walked in. He figured that was fate, right?

"I had a client who was filtering my information about Patel's organization. She was killed."

"Okay, and you came to Apex to find out who had killed her?" Hank was scribbling notes like mad.

"No, I came to get help. I was scared I was next, and I didn't know why."

"Why Apex?" Hank seemed willing to ask the weird questions.

"Because it was the best. When I looked it up, that was the agency. And there were bodyguards—I needed that."

"Okay." Hank glanced up, meeting his eyes, then Rey's. "So I need to look at the reviews. See what might catch some-one's eyes. I don't want to rule anything out."

Rey nodded. "I can try and recreate the search for you."

"Thanks. That's a good idea."

James nodded. "I still have all the documentation I had

when we searched up Patel as the culprit. A new set of eyes might help."

And Hank was a smart kitty, for sure. James liked that. Not just a pretty face.

A flush rose in Hank's cheeks not long after his thought.

You're fascinating. And mine.

Working here, angel. Hank was so pleased, though.

I know. It's hot.

Shhh. Hank patted his thigh. "Okay. We'll start with all the documentation. What was in the information from your client, Rey?"

"Work records. Her HR file. I had a hard copy, and I had to return it."

"There's no copy?" Hank asked.

Rey went pink. "There were crocodiles. Ask Dylan."

Hank snorted. "But there must not have been anything that twigged you, since it was a surprise to find her dead."

"It was stupid—HR stuff, I swear. Nothing weird or illegal or anything. Nothing anyone would die over."

"Huh." Hank flipped to another piece of paper, starting a flow chart. "So, you get the file. You return it, she's dead. You go on the run?"

"Yeah. I drive around, I'm scared to go home, and I started stopping anywhere I could get Wi-Fi."

"To look up agencies? Or did you contact someone?" Hank's gaze sharpened.

"I don't remember if I did. I'm pretty solitary, I think. Mostly."

James frowned. "Wasn't there another friend of yours who did information? Didn't you get ahold of him?"

"Oh. Oh, right. Yeah. God...Does that make me terrible, that I'd forgotten?" Rey looked absolutely awful.

"No way." Hank reached to touch the back of Rey's hand.

"I've lost more than one friend, and we tend to push that away."

"I just...it was my fault, you know?" Rey teared up, and it didn't take thirty seconds before Dylan was right there.

"Hey. Hey, what's wrong?"

"I was telling them about—about all the stuff when we met."

"Ah." Dylan gathered Rey up. "You got enough to start with?" He gave James and Hank a look.

"We do." Hank winked.

"I didn't mean to upset him." James felt like shit.

"I know, man, but he needs a break now."

"Yeah. God, what a mess."

Hank shrugged a little. "It's the nature of our jobs. But Rey is a sweetheart, yeah?"

"He's a lover. Him and Kit, but the rest of us?" James shrugged. "Less so."

"I think you're a lover, baby." Hank touched his leg again. "Okay, let's get those files."

James' computer chimed, Rey's email popping up with the records he'd promised. Good man. "Rey is a trouper. Honest. If anything, he was a patsy in all this."

"I know. I can see the pattern. He was the starting point."

"But why?" He didn't understand that part at all.

"I don't know." Hank chewed his lower lip. "But I don't believe in coincidence."

"Okay. So...so okay. Let's follow the thread."

"Yep." Hank printed out all of Rey's information, so James printed his. Then they took up red pens.

They'd figure this out, dammit. They had to. There had to be a common thread. Something they could cut off and burn down so no one could hurt them again. First though, they needed to discover where all this shit led.

"Follow the money, right?" Hank grinned, sharing his thoughts.

"Always. That seems to be the answer to every question." It made him sad, but the truth was the truth.

"Okay. Let's mark these up and see if we come up with any common thoughts."

"You got it." They put their heads together and got to it. Their red pens flew on the sheets of paper, and James leaned on Hank, happy to have him close.

Finally, they kept leading back to one website—a dummy page that redirected to the Apex main site.

Hank nudged James. "What's this, webmaster?"

"Not us. Not ours. Hold on." He chased his tail a bit, looking for the owner of the domain.

Hank was still marking things on Rey's reports. "This all goes in circles."

"Sort of literally. Look. The red—it's making circles."

"Huh." Hank stared. "Are we just crazy?"

"I don't think so. This isn't coincidence."

"No." They both stared at the circles they were running in. "So, it all loops back to what? A spy page? A funnel page?"

"Maybe. I've got us protected to the teeth." At least he thought he did. Maybe he was wrong.

"Okay, well, it's still a good idea to figure out how they got in, right?" Hank was staring at the computer screen now.

"Yeah, I'll tighten security, but if they're in and crouching..." If they were that much better than him, if he'd fucked up that bad—he was going to have to go to Mick.

"Then we take it to the team. Surely if we know what we're dealing with, we can kick it."

"Yeah." A dull horror was beginning to build inside him. Had he done this?

"Hey. Hey, this is slick work, baby. It just looks like a redirect."

"Still. Is this my fault?" Had he let the evil in?

"No. No, this is the fault of whoever is targeting us. No one on the team is responsible for this."

He nodded, but he was afraid it wasn't true. He was going to fall apart, right here.

"Can you go talk to Mick? I need to do—work."

Hank gave him a suspicious look. "If you need some time, babe, I'm good with that, but we should talk to Mick together."

"I'll just...I have to figure this out." He turned to his computer, head full of swirling worry.

"Okay, babe. You call me if you need me. I'm going to check on Rey." Hank was a doll, giving him space.

He dropped his head to his hands. What had he done? James had a tiny meltdown, his whole body shaking, sobs coming from his throat all the way into his chest. If he'd let them in, then he'd hurt them all.

God. What was he going to do?

A knock sounded on his door, so it couldn't be Hank. Hank had more or less moved in.

"Yes?" He didn't even lift his head up.

"Hey, kiddo." Mick came in, and he didn't know if Hank had said, or if Mick's sixth sense was on fire.

"I—" He looked up at Mick, and suddenly he couldn't breathe. "I'm sorry. I never meant to."

"Hey." Mick rushed him, hugging him up tight. "Hey, you didn't do anything."

"But what if I fucked up, hurt us somehow?"

"You think I don't wonder that every day?" Mick patted his back, oddly comforting, the old mother hen.

"I swear to god, Mick. I'd never do anything on purpose."

"I know that. I know it." Mick lowered him back to the couch. "Hell, I thought I made this place impenetrable, and those weasels got in. How? What did I do wrong? I think it all the time."

"How can we beat someone so much smarter than we are?" He was used to being weaker, to being leaner, but he was also used to being smarter.

"I'm not sure they're smarter." Mick blew out a breath. "First, we weren't expecting them. Then they divided and conquered. They got us running around and working to keep our asses intact. I'm sick of whoever this is being in front of us."

"Me too." He met Mick's eyes. "I swear by my tail, I would never have let them in."

"I know that, kiddo. I do." Mick chuffed a little. "Now we figure out who it is and kick ass."

"Yeah. Yeah, okay." He let himself hug Mick hard. "I love it here. You're my family."

"Good. We love you too, and I'm glad Hank is here for you." Mick just held on. The big guy was a softy.

"I'm worried about Brock. I'm scared someone's going to hurt him."

"Because he's not with us," Mick said seriously.

"Yes. Yes, because he's alone out there." And these people —whoever they were—were smart and vicious.

"Well, Griz gives him some good help." Mick winked, then sobered. "I'm going to call him, see if he'll come back."

"That would be good. All of us together in the same spot." All of them.

"Yeah. I think so. I mean, I know it's been weird." Mick sighed. "I worry."

"Me too." He relaxed into Mick, and he could feel Hank, finally having enough, needing to be the one that comforted him.

"Is he on his way up?" Mick asked, easing away.

"He is. You can tell, huh?"

"Yeah." Mick chuckled. "You two vibrate. You did okay, huh? You didn't do anything wrong." Standing, Mick stretched. "I'll pull Brock in."

"Thank you. For coming up. Seriously."

"Anytime, kiddo." Mick waved, then headed out, passing Hank on his way in.

Hank paused, looking at Mick. "We good?"

Mick nodded. "Golden." He closed the door behind him.

"Sorry." He wasn't sure what he was apologizing for, but he was.

"Why? I was going to talk to Dylan and Mick saw me. I guess I looked like a thundercloud." Hank came right to him.

"I was panicking." He pushed into Hank's arms, launching himself up and trusting that his mate would catch him.

"I know. I just wanted to let you breathe, but I'm here." Hank kissed his neck.

He nodded, and he understood, but now he needed a little care, to be held.

Hank drew him down on the couch, into Hank's lap, those strong arms holding him tight. Yeah, that was it.

"I was so...I thought I was going to have to leave."

"Oh, baby. Mick would never kick you out. The guys told me how hard he had to work to get you to move in." Hank chuckled.

"I just...I would never hurt any of us. I swear. I swear I wouldn't."

"Hey." Hank stroked his cheek. "I know that. I bet that's what Mick said too."

He nodded and held on, his soul shaken.

Hank stopped trying to talk him out of his panic and held him close, loving on him with little snuggles and chuffs. Yes. Talking could be overrated.

He nuzzled in, chirruping softly, calling to Hank's soul.

They cuddled in, and before he could blink they were naked, then shifting, vocalizing to each other. Really, comfort came down to the most basic, cellular level, and like this, so much was clear. They were together and safe in this space that smelled like them now.

They lay nose to tail to nose, Hank grooming him a little. The soothing motion of that rough tongue was a wonder. He felt it from the tips of his claws to tops of his ears. His entire body relaxed, but more importantly, his heartache eased, Hank filling him with peace.

James closed his eyes, breathing deep. *Do you think he can get Brock home?*

Shh. Being kitties. No man talk. Hank nipped at his ear.

"Rowl!" That was mean. A little hot, maybe, but mean.

Hank chuffed again, that kitty laugh making him bat out with his paw. He nuzzled in, blowing his lips against Hank's ruff.

They almost rolled off the couch teasing each other, Hank just catching him with one front paw. The idle strength in his bobcat was surprising and wonderful in the same breath.

His tail snapped, but not because he was unhappy. More for balance, and Hank bit at it.

He chuffed softly, teasing, playing along. They finally did roll off the couch, but landed on their feet, then tore around the apartment for a few minutes.

Then they crashed onto the bed, bouncing hard.

Hank mock growled, pouncing on him, whiskers twitching, and he swiped gently, rumbling with his happiness.

They played, rolling across the whole bed, then back. He chased Hank's tail, nipping and loving on it, batting it back and forth. Hank was obsessed with his ears, which were not near as lovely as Hank's, and with his belly.

Hank's ears had amazing tufts, so pretty, so fuzzy. He licked at one, and swore he could hear laughter.

Hank made it—everything—better.

I want to help. I love you so much already.

James stopped, his whole body stilling. He held Hank's gaze. *Love? You mean it?*

I do. Those eyes flashed gold.

I do too. He had meant it for days.

Good. Hank rubbed cheeks with him, sharing scent and care. His eyelids got heavy, his world spinning lazily.

They flopped down together, curling up, grooming a little more before just settling in, purring.

He relaxed, melting down into the sheets with a happy sigh.

They could sleep now. Maybe they would be more ready to find shit out when they woke up.

If not, he send someone to bring Brock to just come home instead of asking.

SEVEN

Hank went looking for food in the common room, which was becoming a regular thing. He was getting so damn spoiled, just walking down there and having food and drink appear.

And friends. Every one of the guys treated him like a member of the team. Like family.

"Hank! Breakfast burritos." Kit winged a foil-wrapped packet at him. "Dylan was looking for you."

"Yeah? He in his office?"

"He was headed that way." Kit beamed, then brought him a steaming cup of coffee. "No tossing this."

"No, no, that would be awkward."

"Scalding too." Kit winked.

"So—"

Kit titled his head. "You can ask. What do I do besides food?"

"Well, I wasn't going to put it that way."

Kit hooted. "I'm patient. I do a lot of surveillance. I search through camera footage. I drive."

"He tears off heads once in a while." Mick came through. "Ooh, burritos."

"Bacon and egg." Kit handed two off, the bear's eyes following Mick.

"Thanks, kiddo. You going to see Dylan? I'll come with you."

Hank wondered if Mick would ever see Kit like Kit needed him to. He hoped so. They could both use it.

"Sure. Kit says he's hunting me."

Mick unwrapped one burrito, taking a huge bite. Hank winked at Kit as they left, getting a cheery wave.

"Dylan's going to be jealous," he muttered.

"Are you kidding? Dylan was in the kitchen first."

"Oh." He chuckled. "Well, at least I'm not the last one up." Actually, he knew James was up and sneaking in some free weights.

"No, that would be Rey. He's nocturnal."

"Right." Yeah, and foxes seemed to have a harder time with fighting those animal instincts than the rest of them.

Mick knocked on Dylan's office door and opened it. "Hey, man."

"Boss. Hank. Have a seat."

Mick rolled his eyes. "There are chairs in here?"

"Just clear something off." Dylan grabbed a stack of folders. "So, I did some calling around. Hit up some of the guys I used to work with, a few old informants. Trying to find connections between Patel and Hetrick you know?"

"Yeah?" Hank sat, pulling the ubiquitous notebook out of his pocket.

"Yep. Thing is, every one of them says the same thing. Everyone they talk to is nervous. Clammed up. Scared, even."

"Scared? Patel's in jail? How much control can he still have?"

"They're both in jail," Mitch barked. "So who's pulling the puppet strings? There has to be someone to be scared of."

Hank nodded slowly. "I was working the scattered remains of the drug ring before you guys came and got me, and I have to tell you, I can't see how they could do anything on their own. They were morons."

He didn't think they could find their own asses with a handful of fishhooks.

Dylan sighed. "Things are weird out there. People are disappearing too."

"Disappearing? Is there a pattern? Anything that links the victims?"

"Yeah." Dylan flipped pages in his own notebook. "Warehouse owners. Drug dealer. Small-time actress model. Security company owner. Get this. He was known for hiring out croc shifters."

"I don't even know where to find goddamn croc shifters to hire!" Mick sounded frustrated as fuck.

"Do you want to?" Dylan asked mildly.

"No, I just want to know why we didn't know this shit before."

"I think we did know, but we didn't know it was important."

"Yeah." Hank could see that. "This is the first time all the information is coming together."

"So we need to get all this to James and Rey. They're the guys who can put all this in the computer and make connections." Mick sighed and shook his head. "They find a pattern, and we'll have someone to go kill."

"Is Rey good with that, Dylan? I know he was pretty upset."

"He will be. I mean, James doesn't mind if I sit with him, and I don't mind if you hang with James. We're here to make things easier for them."

"Cool." Hank shrugged. Dylan knew his man. "Well, let's get them on it."

"What can I do?" Kit asked from the doorway. "I'm pretty good at watching, gathering intel."

"Do you want to start on the paper part with me, Kit?" Mick asked. "I could use some help."

"Sure." Kit brightened visibly. "Anything I can do."

"Good deal. You and me, we'll pound paper."

Hank thought Kit might just explode. He looked so tickled. One day, Mick would get his head out of his ass. Probably not today, but at least he'd made the offer, so he had to be smarter than the average wolf, right?

Mick and Kit took what had to be a thousand pounds of paperwork from Dylan's office, leaving them alone. "You want to come up to the guys's office?"

"Yeah. I do." Dylan sighed and grinned. "I know they're not weak, either one of them, but I need to be there, I need to be with him."

"Hey, I'm starting to get that." Hank winked.

"Yeah. For you, it's new. That's harder."

"Is it? I'm stupid for James, man." They headed up toward James and Rey's office.

"It eases up. Not the stupidity, that's eternal, but the constant need. It seems to flare when they're scared or in trouble."

"Oh, good to know." It was. The panic set in so fast if James even teetered when he was walking.

"I swear to god, Rey sees a scary movie with Kit, and I'm running."

"But he likes them?"

Dylan snorted. "God yes, but they make his heart race."

"That may be the cutest thing I've ever heard. Seriously."

"Uh-huh." Dylan snorted. "I'm a giant dork."

"But you care for him." That was clear.

"I need him like oxygen."

"That's a little scary to me." Hank gave Dylan a wry grin. "But also cool as hell."

"Sure. It's a whole new worldview." Dylan winked at him.

They walked into the office where Rey and James were tapping furiously at keyboards, but Rey looked up when they walked in, his smile bright and amazing and all for Dylan.

Hank was jealous, for about three seconds before James looked up, beaming at him. "Hank!"

"Hey." He stopped short of the "baby". For now. "You guys working hard?"

"We are. Come have a seat?" *Touch me? I miss you. I need you.*

Hank moved to James' side, the invisible string between them pulling tight. James leaned in, nuzzling him quietly.

Hank wanted to purr. He touched James' hand, watching the fingers curl into something close to claws.

"Did you need something, or are you just here to visit?"

"I wanted to see Rey." Dylan stroked his fox's back lightly. So sweet.

"And I needed to see you." He winked at his lion. "We've got work to do."

"We do." James gave him determined face, and he leaned forward and stole a kiss, because he just had to. Seriously.

James beamed at him when he pulled back. "Hi."

"Hey. Can we work in here with you two?" Hank didn't want to leave the guys alone.

"Absolutely." Rey leaned on Dylan.

"Hell, yes." James patted his leg, then focused back on the screen.

"The files I sent up need to be—"

"Compiled and compared. Yes, mate. We're on it." Rey leaned against Dylan and typed.

"So we're here for decoration?" Dylan murmured.

"Protection, advice," James offered.

"Moral support. Morale, too." Rey chuckled, typing madly.

"Periodic snuggles, Foxy," James said. "Those are important."

"So much." Joy swelled in Hank's chest at how happy James seemed.

"Yeah, yeah, yeah. Can you cross-check where the stripper model/actress worked?"

"You got it." He could work like a dog when he needed to.

"Good deal. I think Patel owed the bar she danced in."

His pulse kicked up a notch. Every connection got them closer to solving things. "Do you have a board in here we can use?"

"I have a huge screen and mind mapping software." The screen came up, and James started adding pictures and circles and lines.

"Thanks, baby." High tech, but Hank could adapt. He put up the club where the lady in question had worked, then Patel's name. All he needed was for James to approve the line between.

They started moving, drawing connections. Patel had a thumb in a surprising number of the disappeared people.

"So." Hank stood back, hands on his hips. "Should I try to get an interview with Patel?"

"If you do, I'm coming with." Dylan sounded so sure.

"Okay. We can pull good cop-bad cop."

Dylan snorted. "I get to be bad cop. He put my fox in a cage."

"I want to know if he dabbled in the drug trade."

"I don't think he did. That seems to be all Hetrick." James sighed and shook his head.

"Well, it can't hurt to grill him again," Dylan said, a little too gleeful. "I have a couple of friends at the prison."

"He has friends all over. It's a thing of beauty." Rey gave him this amazing grin.

"Brock is like that. He knows everyone." James winked at him.

Hank raised his hands. "I was undercover. I can't admit to knowing anyone."

"You knew Brock, and that was enough."

"Truth." He'd never been more grateful for anything.

"Did Brock know Patel?" Rey asked, and James frowned. "Why would he?"

"He would have told us," Rey said, scowling.

"It's worth asking. I want to know where the connections are, that's all."

"I'll call him." James stared them all down. "He'll be insulted."

"You can just ask him for his eyes on this. He'll be able to put something together." Hank wasn't interested in hurt feelings.

"That will work." Dylan met James' glare head on.

"He's my brother, my best friend. He's not lying to me!"

"I never said he was!" Hank growled. "I just think someone needs to ask. You want me to, he's not gonna get all butthurt."

Dylan and Rey watched them, wide-eyed. "Meow."

"Hush, you two." Hank stared back at James, who finally blew out a breath.

"Come with me. We'll call him together."

"That I can work with."

James nodded and took his hand. "Sorry, mate. I just know he would never betray me. Ever."

"Then we'll ask him to help us." Brock was key here. Hank trusted his gut, but he had no idea what it all meant.

Brock was the answer.

"I will. You know him. He's good."

"Brock? Is loyal. Fierce. Strong." Not good. It took a certain amount of moral flexibility to do wet work. Brock had that. James had a blind adoration for the man, which was dear, but also ridiculous.

They started on the way down, leaving Rey and Dylan behind. The two of them were already in a clench, Dylan pushing away Rey's worry.

"Don't be jealous," James murmured. He thought James was teasing, trying to make up for snapping.

"I don't have to be." He saw the hurt pop up in eyes, and he continued, "I trust you. Totally."

"Oh." James took his hand, nuzzled it.

He hummed, then turned his hand to touch James' cheek. This was what was important, balls-deep.

"I just get defensive. Like Mick, in my own way. The team is my life."

"And now, it's my life. We're working together, angel."

"We are." James laughed. "Okay. I'll be good."

"Nah. I'm a bobcat. I'm stubborn. We'll snarl. What you need to be is willing to forgive, which I think you are."

"Maybe. Maybe a little." James winked at him. "Let me get hold of Brock."

"Sure, baby." He flopped on James' couch, watching his lover get out of the chair and walk. He was getting better at it every day. Hank couldn't wait for James to show the whole crew.

James brought his phone and settled, moving a little stiffly, but so much better. "I'm going to put him on speaker."

"Works for me. Make sure he knows." He didn't want Brock surprised if he cut in.

"Sure. No lies, right?" James pressed his phone, and when the growly, low voice sounded, James said, "It's me, brother. You're on speaker."

"Hey, *doce*. What's wrong?" Brock sounded like he'd been asleep.

"Did you know Patel? In any way? I'm trying to put these lines together, and... I need help." James' voice sounded... scared.

"No. I mean, not that I know of."

"What?" James scowled.

"I did jobs for years that I took through an intermediary. I can't guarantee I didn't work for him at some point, but I doubt it, or he wouldn't have come after us. I had a reputation."

"Almost everything comes back to Patel and Hetrick. I've...I think it's somehow about you. Somehow, brother. I'm worried."

"About me." Brock sighed instead of protesting. "Don't think it hasn't crossed my mind. I just can't see how it all adds up."

"I don't either, but we have to figure it." James shook his head. "We have to."

"We do." Brock paused. "Let me talk to Griz. I'll call you back tonight."

"Be careful. I have this feeling..." James looked so stressed.

"We're fine, worrywart."

"Okay, but you know I'm rarely wrong."

Hank reached for James. He would have to talk to his lover about these feelings.

"Uh-huh. Go play with your new mate, *irmão*. Stop thinking about work."

Hank raised an eyebrow. He wasn't sure what to make of that.

"I can't. I have to fix this, brother."

Brock blew out a breath. "Yeah. Well. I'll talk to Locke, maybe make a few calls. I'll ring in a bit, no?"

"Thank you. Take care of yourself."

"You too, *doce*." Brock hung up, and Hank waited to see how James reacted to the conversation.

He'd found it a tiny bit less than satisfying.

"He doesn't believe me."

"I'm not sure that's it. I think he wants to be cautious." Hank thought Brock as super cagey.

"I—Yeah. Yeah. Do you think I'm crazy?"

"No, baby. In fact, as an outsider, I say there's a definite pattern." Hank wasn't blowing smoke. There was something going on here.

"I think so too. I think this is broken."

"Well, if Griz thinks you're right, I bet you hear back sooner than Brock thinks." Bears had a great sense of danger. And there was no way Griz would let Brock be too reckless.

Hank understood that far more today than he had a few days ago. He had this deep-seated need to protect James. To assure his lover was defended and adored.

He would go to the end of the earth to do just that.

James glanced at him and smiled, eyes heated and happy. Hank had to smile back, then move closer to his lover, reaching out to hold his hand.

"If you kiss me, I'm going to lose my train of thought."

"Is that bad?" Hank grinned, waiting to see what James wanted.

"God, no. It's not bad at all." eyes twinkled at him.

"Kisses are on the menu, then."

"If Rey gets Dylan, then I can have you."

"That's good logic." He leaned over to kiss James' mouth, and James opened up to him easy as pie.

The kiss went deep, the soft press of lips and harsh scrape of tongues making him moan. That was what he needed, what made him feel good. Touching James was such a revelation for a loner like Hank.

Not anymore. Now he was part of something. Now he knew where he belonged.

James stroked the back of Hank's neck, fingers super gentle. The caress was almost a tickle, almost a scratch, but somehow neither of those things. Hank trilled a little, his bobcat right there on the edge of his consciousness. Scratches did that to him.

James' eyes lit pure gold from the usual green at the sound, and that gave Hank all the shivers. He reached up to touch James' cheek.

"Damn, baby. You make me all growly."

"You make me want to purr." James nuzzled in, the motion as old as time.

"Good." That was no complaint. He kinda thought James loved how Hank made him feel.

"Yes." James cuddled in, scenting his throat, nose pushing against his neck. The motion gave him chill bumps, his body on high alert.

Hank slid a hand into James' hair, holding him close. His mate began to lick, the deep purrs and chirrups vibrating his entire body. All he could do was lean into it, luxuriating in James' care. There was nothing else on earth like the touch of his mate, and he could sit there all day. In fact, he kind of wanted to. How did anyone at Apex get anything done? Lord.

James chuckled. "It was like...like a landslide. First Dylan. Then Brock. Now me. We're all mating and..."

James pulled back, eyes going wide. "What if that's on purpose? What if they're trying to distract us?"

"What?" Hank blinked. "How can it be on purpose? I mean, okay, Griz and Brock I can see, but how on earth would they know?"

"The drugs? Did it start something fake?"

Hank could sense James utter panic.

He growled, holding James tight. "Does this feel fake to you?" He set his teeth to James' neck.

James clung to him, panting. "No. Not one bit. It just seems so—how can it be a coincidence?"

"I bet it happens a lot. Pheromones." He didn't care. He didn't give a shit. James was his. James cared enough to find him, bring him here, dream about him. "You dreamed about me. We're mates."

"I did." James soothed, him probably without thinking, hands smoothing over his body.

"You did, and I need you. Like I need the next breath."

"Love." James kissed him, and if there was a little desperation in it, well, Hank wasn't going to mention it. He wanted to make sure James knew he was there for him, because of him. Not because some freaky super villain was playing games.

And it didn't matter to him how they'd mated, not a bit. James was his. He would bet Dylan and Brock would say the same about their mates.

He pushed James down to climb on top of him, needing to touch and love.

Those lovely eyes blinked up at him, the arousal in them clear as day.

"Damn you're pretty." James revved his engine like nothing else ever had. Which made sense. He took another kiss, then another.

"Glad you think so. You want me?"

"Hell, yes. I want to fuck you, baby. So bad." He needed to make sure his lover understood how he felt.

"I'm here and yours. Let's do it." James wasn't teasing, wasn't playing.

He nodded, and they got down to getting naked. Sadly, he had to roll off James to do it, and he mourned the contact. Still, soon enough he and James were bare and coming back together, skin on skin.

"Is this normal? How much I need you? How much I ache for you?" James asked.

"I think so. Dylan says it is."

"So long as we're together. Touch me."

Hank gave up on talking, loving on James with his hands and mouth, with his whole body. His lion arched, responding immediately.

They moved together, rubbing, skin on skin, their scents intermingling. James moaned, and the worry that buzzed under his skin disappeared like a bubble popping. God, that felt good, to be able to make James so happy. He felt like a hero, like he was something else, something special.

Hell, he felt ten feet tall and bulletproof.

They panted, sharing kiss after kiss. Then he had to bite a little like the kitty he was.

"Fuck. More."

Oh, that made him grin. "Or more fucking?" He had to. The opening was clear.

"I will bite you." James clicked his teeth together near Hank's nipple.

"Promise?" Marking each other sounded like a fine thing.

Those green eyes flashed to him. "Swear."

Then lips fastened above his nipple. The shock of the suction had him bucking, the skin where James was sucking tingling hard. His nipple went hard as a rock, like it was screaming for attention.

He put one hand behind head, fingers digging into that heavy hair, and James pulled harder, teeth sliding on his skin. It was enough to drive him out of his fucking mind, and he rowled softly, the sound pure hunger.

"More?" James was chuckling, breathless and happy.

"More." His skin tingled, his balls pulling up.

James licked and bit, making a trail across to the same spot over his other nipple.

Moaning, he felt the flames lick through his body, making him fly. He'd never once had a lover so focused on him, on his needs. James made him bare his teeth, made him wild. No wonder Brock felt the need to get out of town.

No one could work and mate at the same time.

"Focus." James nipped harder, making his nipple sting.

"I am, baby. Trust me. I'm only thinking about you."

"Good, because I need you like food or water."

"Uhn." The words really revved his engine. God, this man made him crazy.

James was relentless, sucking and licking and groaning as that mouth worked. Hank twisted and moaned, trying to get more. Fuck, yes.

"Good. Gonna slick you up before you take me."

"Uh-huh, okay." His overheated brain really wasn't capable of much more. Dylan promised him this wild need would ease, but it hadn't yet, and Hank wanted to enjoy every second.

The whole "take me" concept kind of sent him into paroxysms of lust.

James' mouth dropped over his cock like a lead balloon, surrounding him with pure heat.

All he could do was stare at James and stroke that heavy hair and wonder at his amazing life. That and make sure he didn't shoot—because his mate wanted a good, hard plugging.

That he would be happy as hell to provide.

James pulled hard, swallowing around his cock.

"Baby. If you want me you fuck you, I'm plenty wet. I'm gonna come, you don't stop."

Those bright eyes met his as James pulled off with a pop. "I need you."

"Good. Get up here, huh?" He wanted James on his cock. Fuck that, he needed it.

James climbed up along his body, kissing and licking along

the way. That was a fine thing, and he stroked every bit of skin he could reach as James flowed over him.

James spread, tiny hole opening around the tip of his cock.

"Oh, damn." Hank grabbed that ass, a cheek in each hand.

"Good?" James took him in to the root.

"Oh, honey. Better than good. You're fucking perfect." He tugged James down, then lifted him up, loving how strong his mate was becoming. Those thighs were contracting and pulling, working with him now.

Yeah. They were cooking with oil. They were rocking together, his cock sinking into James over and over.

"Harder. Mate, I ache for you." The soft words started a fire in the pit of his gut.

Hank moved faster, harder, slamming into James, and he rejoiced in the way James pushed back onto him. He would never get enough of this man. Never.

"Love the way you feel, honey."

"Yes. Love. I need you." face was wild. Beautiful.

"Got me. Anything." Sweat dripped off his face, his breath heaving in his chest, and when lips crashed down on his, he lost any semblance of humanity. He was all growls and instinct, moving in a haze of need. James met him with bites and yowls, the sounds driving him higher.

His body arched and worked like a piston, back and forth, driving him on, and all the while James rode him, slapping them together.

"Come on, baby. Right on the edge." He reached for that hard cock, wanting to touch.

"Yes." The low growl settled in the pit of his stomach, making his own cock swell even more.

"Damn. Oh, damn, James."

"Hank. Now. Now, mate." James' body squeezed his cock tight.

His head snapped back, his hips rising like a tidal wave as he shot inside James. "Yes! James!"

Heat poured over his fingers, the sweet sound of mind filling his head. The pleasure washed through him, doubled with what he got from his lover.

Mate. Ache for you. You make me need. Sweet mate.

He nodded, then drew James down to him for a kiss. He needed it now, the warm, slow slide of lips and tongues.

"Mick's going to beat us, all being in bed twenty-four seven."

"Is he?" He pondered that. Mick probably could kick his ass, but Hank thought the big guy understood the mating game, even if he was still single. It sucked that they were all doing it in order. Hell, he'd probably beat Dylan.

James grinned. "Yeah. But he's never really beaten anyone except at the gym. He's a good man, like all the way to the bone. It's a little bit scary, really."

Hank snorted. "I bet. I'm a cop. Think how few good people I know."

"Do you like it? Did you, I mean? Being a policeman?"

Hank tilted his head. "Yeah. I liked being a cop until I started doing undercover and got picked up by the feds. Then it became a tough row to hoe."

"I think it would be hard to lie all the time about who you were."

"It was. It makes a man tired." He shook it off a little. "I was so glad Mick offered me a job."

"Yes. I dreamed about you. I need you."

"Mmm." He stroked cheek. "I'm here now. We're together. Love."

"Love." James beamed at him. "Together."

"Life has never been better, baby. Even with the weird."

"Yeah, we'll figure the weird. We will. I just have to work out the connections. There has to be one."

"There does. We need to get Brock in here and talk to him." He hated to harp on it.

"Yeah, if we can. He's stubborn."

"I know, but he'll come if you ask. I know he will."

"Yeah. Yeah, I'll ask him. He needs to come home."

Hank hugged James because he sounded a little miserable now, which he hated. Still, this team needed to stop being fractured.

James met his eyes. "You're right. We need to be in one place to be safe—except we weren't. We weren't safe together."

"I know." He shook his head. "This is all about y'all somehow. I just don't know how."

"Me either." James held him. "But we have to figure it out."

That was true in the most basic way, so he just nodded. "But not this minute."

"No. This minute is ours."

"Just us, baby. Just this right now." Hank could go with that.

"Yes." James closed his eyes, lashes tickling Hank's shoulder.

"Love you." That seemed like the most important thing.

"Thank the moon."

Hank felt his mate relaxing, melting down against him. They wrapped together, sinking into the bed. They could rest. Heal even more.

Breathe and focus.

———

James was going to get out of the fucking chair. He couldn't fix anything else, he couldn't think, he couldn't reach Brock, so he got on the treadmill and forced himself to walk.

After a few minutes he was sweating, but there was no

pain in his back or hips, so he kept on. He held himself up with his arms, demanding that his stupid legs function.

They were working, if slow and kind of wonky. That was something, right?

It wasn't until about twenty minutes in that he realized he didn't know how he was supposed to stop.

"Uh. Help?" He wheezed out the word, breathing too hard to shout. *Mate? Mate, I'm stuck.*

Coming! Where are you! Hank was on it, startled.

Treadmill. He was beginning to panic.

Twenty seconds.

James counted. One. Two. Three.

His arms shook, but he would manage to wait. He had to.

Hank burst in seconds later, racing to snatch him off the treadmill.

"Mate." He held on, trembling like an autumn leaf.

"I got you, baby. I do." Hank was a solid chunk of a man, little as he was, holding James up easily.

"Sorry. I was walking." He was trying to grow stronger.

"That's fab, but I think you overdid it." At least Hank wasn't laughing at him.

"You think? I was holding myself up, and I didn't have a hand to hit stop." He was an idiot. Lord.

"Well, now you're off." Hank muscled him over to his chair to ease him down, then moved to turn off the treadmill.

He panted softly, muscles bunching and clenching with the release.

"That's it, baby. Just relax."

"Sorry. I feel stupid."

"No, you were doing great. I'll just come work out with you from now on."

A light knock sounded at the gym door before Kit stuck his head in. "Everyone okay?"

"Yeah. He's doing great. He just got a little worn out."

James' cheeks were on fire, but he nodded in agreement.

"Okay. Holler if you need me." Kit disappeared.

"He has radar," James murmured.

"He's an empath, for sure. He'd make one hell of a cop, even though it would break his heart."

James wouldn't have that. Kit deserved a heart that was whole.

"He's a good house mom and he assists everyone with their investigations. He's a great guy, and we need an admin with Carrie here less and less."

Hank nodded. "I get you."

"You sure do. Thank you." He would have fallen, sure as shit.

"No problem, baby." Hank came over to bend down for a kiss. "You are killing it. You're going to leave that chair behind."

"I walked down here holding the handles." He grinned, allowing himself to be proud.

"That's my mate. So fucking strong. I'm so proud."

His chest swelled a little, his breath catching up and getting oxygen to his brain. "Sorry. God, I just got overwhelmed."

"Hey, it happens." Hank got them moving, wheeling him out of the gym.

"Yeah, I guess. I'm not much of a gym guy." He was more of a live in the cave with lots of coffee and his huge screen guy.

"I like naps and short bursts of activity. We're cats, baby."

"We are." Hank was very much a cat, more than he was in many ways. Then again, James could go for days without seeing anyone, and he loved tuna...

"And cream. You could lap cream off my cock."

He blinked up into Hank's eyes. "Yes. Yes, I so could."

"Now is probably bad, as wiped as you are." Hank winked down at him.

"I was talking theoretical, dork." They cracked up, laughing hard together.

Hank kissed the top of his head. "Okay. Let's get you clean."

He nodded, but he wasn't sure he could stand up on his own two feet once they got upstairs.

You don't have to. You can rest.

I can. What were you doing?

Hank chuckled. *Reading files.*

When you could have been admiring my sexy ass? Man…

Such a waste of time. Hank caressed the back of his neck. "Did you figure anything out in your research?"

"I'm just making another pin board at this point."

James chuckled softly. "Such a cop."

"I am. I'm not as old school as Dylan."

"I like it. You. Your mind works in an amazing way."

"Thank you, baby." Hank detoured at the office level, and he had a feeling his sweaty ass was about to see the pinboard.

At least he'd be dried off and ready for his shower by the time Hank was done showing off.

Hank wheeled him into the office, and sure enough, someone had moved a big bulletin board in, where Hank had posted pictures and words and string connections.

In the center of it all was a picture of Brock, the dark eyes seeming to stare into him. He would accuse Hank of being obsessed, but when he started looking, all the strings actually led there.

"So he's the why. We have one answer." They needed to make sure Brock was safe. Because if it was all about Brock, then the target was off Apex's back. It was harder to hit eight men than one.

"We need to get a hold of him, hon. He and Griz need to know."

"Yes. Now. You showed this to Mick yet?"

Hank shook his head, chewing his lip. "I didn't want to bother him."

James chuckled. "Upset him you mean. Go get him. I'll call Brock."

It was time to stop fluttering about this shit. He needed his soul brother and the bear home. They needed to gather around and get shit done. Someone had split them and confused them, but they were stronger together.

Hank nodded, then bent to kiss him before heading off.

He rolled himself over and closed the door, then sent the text letting Brock know to call. He included a pic of the pin board. It didn't take long before his phone rang and he answered. "You have to come home. You're not safe."

"Hey. Slow down, *doce*. What's going on now?" Brock's voice took on a concerned tone rather than a humor the lunatic one, which was good.

"This whole thing—it points back to you. Come home where we can be a pride. At least together..." What? They'd already fucked this up bad, hadn't they?

Brock chuckled, the sound wry. "At least we'll know where everyone is."

"And we'll be a family. I worry about you. Us. All of us."

"I know, *irmão*. I know we shouldn't have run off. But we needed bonding time."

"I understand, but I have a feeling. I think...I think someone's coming for you."

"Okay. We'll come home, then. I trust you." Brock's accent deepened like it always did when something was important.

"Thank you. Take care. We're waiting for you." Thank goodness.

Brock chuckled. "Impatient lion."

"Yes, brother. I want you to know my Hank."

"I want to see you walk. You're trying, right?" Brock sounded wistful.

"I just got off the treadmill."

"No shit?"

James snorted. "It almost killed me, but I did it."

"Fucking A, *mi irmão*! That's the way." Brock's pride filled James right up.

"Thanks. Hank has really lit a fire under my ass."

"You hooked up with a bobcat beat cop..."

"I did. And I used to tease Rey about being with Dylan." That was irony, and James knew it. "And he was undercover. Not a beat cop."

"Right. And a Fed at the end not a cop..." Brock sighed, but it wasn't unhappy, he thought. "We'll be back soon."

"Thank you. We're going to be stronger together." He needed to believe that. He had to.

"I trust your gut, James. I do. Let me get Griz and see how he wants to do this, logistics-wise. I will text you an ETA."

"Thank you. I'll be waiting." Hopefully he'd done well. He hung up, waiting for Hank and Mick to come back.

"Look. I'm sure you think you're on to something, Hank, but I—" Mick entered the room, trailing off when he saw the board. "Damn."

"He's coming home. I contacted him."

"Good." Mitch's gaze swept the board. "Goddamn it. I hate being behind the curve."

Kit sighed from the doorway. "Are you sure he's safer here? Maybe we should all scatter."

James shook his head. "I know we really haven't done so well so far, but I have a bad feeling."

Kit's dark brown eyes stared him down. "Are you sure? I'm worried."

"I'm as sure as I can be." James shrugged. "I have as much to lose as anyone, bud. I wouldn't get us all here on a whim."

"No. No, you never would." Kit's entire body relaxed, and didn't that feel amazing? Didn't that feel good?

"Thanks." He motioned to the board. "So who did Brock piss off?"

"Someone who is smart enough to set all this up, from the start," Mick said. "Kit, honey, get Dylan and Rey."

"On it." Kit left them, and James chuckled.

"I'm a little sweaty."

Hank grinned. "You don't stink."

Mick arched an eyebrow. "Working out?"

"Yes. Getting healthier every day."

"Good deal." Mick beamed at him, looking so proud.

"I need to be strong for this—wheels or not."

"We all do," Hank murmured.

Mick nodded, chewing his cheek as he looked at the board. "So he's in the middle of a shitstorm—we have Patel, Hetrick, and we have the weasels as the main players?"

"Yeah. The crocs worked for Patel."

"Didn't the weasels work for Hetrick?"

"They did." Hank nodded slowly. "Jesus. And both major players were happy to go to jail. Because they failed to get Brock?"

"That doesn't make sense. Who's scarier than jail?"

Mick shook his head. "Some kind of criminal mastermind?" The sarcasm was deafening.

"Like Moriarty?" Kit came in with Rey and Dylan.

"Who?" Dylan asked.

"Sherlock Holmes' nemesis. Kit's being sarcastic, love."

Dylan rolled his eyes. "Kit reads too much."

"Not possible," Kit shot back.

"Says the man who reads ten mysteries a week. Dylan just likes James Patterson."

James had to grin. This was his team. Here. Fired up.

"What about you, babe? What do you read?"

James grinned. "I like Stephen King. Are you shocked?"

"Not one bit." Hank winked broadly. "You like the scary. Such a kitty."

"Meow." He wanted to rub their noses together, so bad.

Hank did, leaning down to give him scent and breath. No one said a thing, so James hummed, a happy noise for his mate. He closed his eyes, purring deep in his chest.

Mick finally did clear his throat. "So, what next?"

"Now we keep making lines. Eventually one of them will cross." Hank sounded so sure.

"Okay. I brought my notes from all the calls I made," Dylan said.

"I brought our tablets, James." Rey handed him his, and he grinned.

"Brill, man. Simply brill."

"Thanks." Rey beamed, and James nodded.

Time to get shit done.

It was about fucking time.

Eight

Hank watched the strings go up on the board, the web enormous and a little overwhelming. Shit, this was a full-on conspiracy.

Once James had taken the step and demanded that Brock come home, it was like his mate could think again, one idea coming after the other.

Brock was supposed to arrive today. But the whole team was beating the pavement. Hell, Dylan was trying to get a new interview with Patel.

"So we all agree the weasels are just hired hands and we can shunt them to the side?" James asked.

"I think so, yeah." Hank searched the board. "They show up once, they have one connection to Hetrick and his weird drug cult."

"Fine." Rey moved the pins and put the weasels to the side.

"Now, Patel has all these properties and shit." Dylan waved at the board. "And he has an investment or two with Hetrick."

"Is there a connection with the serpents and the crocodiles?"

"Aside from Patel?" Mick studied the board.

Dylan's phone began to ring, and he grabbed it. "'Lo?"

Before he even said a word, the look on the wolf's face made them all tense.

"Uh-huh. Okay. Thanks so much for letting us know." Dylan hung up, then blew out a gusty breath. "Patel escaped. Like half an hour after I called to get a damn interview with him."

Rey went totally gray, ashen. "I—"

"Shh." Dylan tugged Rey into his arms. "We've got some warning."

"No one will let him get to you." James stared at Rey. "Right, Mick?"

"Fucking A." Mick's voice was deadly serious. "I have fucking had enough."

"Okay. We need to be prepared. James, call Brock and get him up to speed." Dylan was just really good at that.

"I'll see if he'll answer." James texted Brock immediately.

"We're on our way, *irmão*. What's up?" Brock called right away, and James put him on speaker.

"Patel escaped."

Hank was fascinated by the immediate worry that ran through the team.

"Well, damn. Batten down the hatches." That had to be Griz. Damn, the man had a deep voice.

"Don't worry, Fox. The bastard knows he can't get you."

Fox.

Hank frowned. Why on earth did Brock call Rey 'fox' like that? He didn't do it for anyone else.

He made a mental note to ask James so he didn't derail the train right now.

"I hope so, Brock." Rey rubbed his arms. "Get here."

"Coming. Soon. Order pizza. I'm craving."

So soon. Tonight.

"I'm on it," James said. "I know what you like."

"You do." The phone line went dead, and he found himself rumbling at the intimate sound of Brock's voice.

James glanced at him. "Hush. It's not like that."

"I know." Still. Grr. He wanted to drag James somewhere and bite him.

James grinned, Mick rolled his eyes, and Kit laughed. "I'll get munchies."

"I'm staying with Dylan." Rey muttered, his long nose working.

"Okay." Kit wandered off. Hank wanted to as well, but Brock was coming, and Mick was in work mode.

"Boss?"

"Yeah?" Mick met his eyes.

"You got a second?"

"You know it." Mick took him out in the hall. "What's up?"

"Why doesn't Brock like Rey?"

"He liked Rey just fine." Mick chuckled, but there was little humor in it. "Now, foxes? He has an issue with."

"Foxes? Why? What's up?"

"Ex situation. Guy convinced him they were mates. Lost Griz over it for a long while apparently." Mick pulled a face. "We're all stupid sometimes."

"Why?" Why act like mates when they weren't? Why push a mate bond out of the way just to fuck with someone?

"I have no idea. Brock is pretty closed mouth about it." Mick shrugged. "That was what I dragged out of him."

"Huh." He needed to talk to his mate. There was something there.

"Yeah. You think it's important?"

Hawk chewed his lip. "I say it's worth asking about again." His gut told him something was here.

"Then ask. That's the way to handle this. Ask the questions. I'm done with this fucking thing."

"Good deal. I will." He could do this. He was the new guy, and a fellow cat. Brock would be more likely to act like he was a stranger. Hell, first he'd just interrogate James.

James raised an eyebrow when they came back into the room.

Dammit. Interrogate was a bad word.

"What do you know about Brock's ex?" Hank asked, knowing he was springing it out of nowhere and watching James closely.

"He hurt Brock a lot. He's a user." James' expression was mild as milk.

"What does he do?"

"He did black ops until—" James trailed off and shook his head.

Black ops. Shit. That could totally be what they were dealing with. "Until?"

"The breakup. The asshole broke Brock's cover, left him to swing in the wind."

"Damn." Hank pondered that, and he could feel every man in the room thinking about it too.

"Yeah. It hurt him—in lots of ways." James slowly stretched. "We took care of it."

"How?" Hank hated asking so many questions, but he needed to know.

James shrugged. *Mate, no.*

Why no? We need to know if this fox is a problem.

I—I can't. It was ugly.

Tell me in a bit? Surely James could say it to just him.

That got him a nod, and he accepted it. That was good enough.

He sat back in his chair, still looking at the board. He had a feeling in his gut, and Hank rarely denied those. If there was a pissed former lover that had access and skills, he could fuck Brock over and stay invisible. That wasn't gonna fly anymore, if that was it.

Of course, now they had to worry about finding Patel, too. He had to know something.

"How did Patel escape?" he asked, and Dylan rolled his eyes.

"A guard let him go."

"What?"

"That's what it looked like on the security cams. A guard just let him go."

"So he bribed someone?" Rey's eyebrows went up and down.

"Or someone paid off the guard because they wanted Patel in the wind." Though the fact that Patel left after he'd maintained he was safer in jail was bizarre.

"It doesn't matter," James looked up at him, expression sick. "The guard's dead."

"Wait. What? How?"

"They found his body in a closet, stabbed to death."

"Shit." Man, this thing just kept getting deeper and deeper, like one of those oubliette things. A hole where someone dropped shit they wanted to hide.

"Is there video we can get hold of?" Dylan asked. "There has to be, right?"

"I'll try." James looked around. Yeah, he needed his computer.

"I need to see it. I'll know if it's Patel."

"Okay." James rolled to the machine he used down here and

cracked his knuckles. Every so often his lover made him dizzy, with how fast his fingers moved. Everyone else seemed to feel the same way except Rey, who stood close to murmur some suggestions.

Suddenly it was like lion and fox were connected, their minds flashing together. Hank could almost hear it, the way they were clicking.

"Like a machine," Mick murmured.

"Techies," Dylan said, rolling his eyes again.

"It's fucking cool, isn't it?" He glanced at Dylan with a wild grin.

"It is." Dylan chuckled. "Seriously. I'm a gumshoe, you know? I beat the pavement."

"I'm an undercover guy. I make weird-assed leaps of logic."

"And hide." Mick gave him a mildly amused look.

"Not anymore. I'm with this team."

"I was fucking with you, man. That's all," Mick said mildly.

"I know. I think I do, anyway. Undercover work makes a man paranoid."

I have you, mate. Always.

Love. Thank you. I push. It's part of me.

He saw James nod, smile, the look fond.

The door opened, making them all jump, Brock and Griz striding into the room.

Brock went right to Hank's mate, brushing their cheeks together.

"Brother. Welcome home."

"Thank you, *irmão*." Brock smiled, and Hank expected to feel jealous. He didn't. "You look good, happy."

"I am. I found my mate."

"Mmm. Hello, Hank." Brock smiled for him, which transformed that serious face.

"Brock. Welcome home."

"Thank you." Brock sighed when he glanced at the board. "Well, look at that."

Lord, were they going to have a meltdown?

Griz made this low growling noise. "Okay, so. What do we do about this?"

"First we find Patel." Rey pursed his lips. "He didn't kill the guard. Look."

Patel was in the video, but the tiger was…

"Is he bound?" Hank leaned forward. "Is he zip-tied?"

"Yeah. Yeah, he can't shift, and he thinks that guy is gonna kill him."

"Never seen a tiger scared before," Locke rumbled. "Who's the other guard then?"

"Some dude dressed like a guard?" Rey said.

James turned to try to make the picture bigger or clearer or something. "It's like he's wearing a mask or something—I can't get any features."

Brock nodded slowly. "There are distortion masks. They're pretty high tech."

There was something in Brock's eyes. Something off.

"How rare would that be?" Hank asked carefully.

Brock glanced at him. "Expensive, more than rare."

Brock knew something. He knew it, and he wasn't sharing. Hank raised an eyebrow, and Brock shook his head, but he didn't look… mean. Just not ready.

The man had just come home, after all.

"How was your retreat?" he asked Locke.

"Productive." Something about the way the big grizzly's eyebrows went up made him chuckle. Lord have mercy. The bear started grinning, and suddenly Dylan was in on it, the wolf's chuffing laughter filling the air.

Hank shook his head, grinning, and James nudged Brock, who snorted. "Awkward."

"But so true." Locke hummed, and suddenly they all looked away and got very busy.

Hank watched Brock work with Rey and James, and it was clear that James was in the center of two storms that moved at different rates. Brock was like a hurricane, all blunt force. Rey was more like... maybe a sandstorm. A dust devil that whirled from one point to another.

No wonder his mate needed serious rest sometimes.

"Dude," Dylan nudged him. "You're growling."

"Huh? Sorry." He ducked his head, but Dylan just grinned. "I get it. I'm fairly newly mated, huh? But Mick is starting to get grumpy."

"Hey, I've been working." Hank waved at the pin board.

"You have. I can't believe we didn't see all this."

Hank shook his head. "It's a huge picture."

"And fucking convoluted," Dylan agreed. "Too many moving parts."

Mick broke in. "We need to find Patel. If he's in the wind, it's for a reason."

"Even if it's a trap?" Brock asked.

"Especially if it's a trap." Hank insisted. "We keep being on the wrong side of the eight ball."

"Right." Mick nodded decisively. "Let me and Dylan know when you find him, lads. We'll go get him."

James nodded absently. "Our best bet is traffic and security cams." His fingers flew on the keyboard.

"Right. I'll work the angle of his properties, but I don't think that'll help, not if he's been kidnapped."

"Anything might help now," Rey murmured.

Mick stood, stretching hugely. "Come on, Dylan. Let's get the armory prepped."

"Just in case there are crocs," Dylan said darkly.

"Crocs." That just blew his goddamn mind.

"Right? I mean, I didn't think anything that primitive could bond with the human to make a shifter." That was Kit, who had obviously given croc shifters a bit of thought. Like, in a deep way.

"I don't even want to imagine...Do they think? I mean, is there someone in there?"

"I have no idea, but some of them had human bodies for a while..." Kit shuddered. "They stank."

Mick rumbled softly. "They didn't get us, cub."

"I know." The glance that Kit gave Mick made him wonder if the boss knew Kit wasn't a cub. He hoped so, but that was none of his nosy business. None.

He had a mate to deal with, after all.

His own mate. Who was starting to droop and who would need rest soon.

Rest meant napping. Napping meant post-nap naked snuggling. Post-nap naked snuggles were a good thing.

Hank thought that sounded so good that he sent an image of it to James, or tried to.

James blinked, head tilting, and then their eyes met.

He grinned, waggling his eyebrows.

"Go, *irmão*," Brock murmured. "I'll help the fox."

"You don't mind."

"*Não*. Go on." Brock reached out to squeeze James' shoulder.

James grabbed Brock up, hugging him tight. "Missed you."

"I missed you too. Now go on." Brock actually winked at Hank, who didn't argue.

He just hopped up to grab the handles of James' chair to wheel him right out of the room. Hank wanted his James and he wanted him now.

"Time to nap, is it?" James was all purrs and rumbles. "I heard you."

"You're looking tired, love. And I wanted to hold you." Mating was exhausting, even if it was amazing.

"Is this where you tell me not to feel guilty for taking a break?"

"Yep. Hell, I need frequent ones myself. I was undercover too long." Hank shrugged when James glanced back at him. "It wears on a man."

"You had to pretend—" eyes went wide, warning in them. "Hank!"

Hank whirled around, immediately taking the hint, and damn if there wasn't a very, very scruffy looking Patel the tiger shifter standing behind him, his face gaunt, his eyes haunted.

Patel held up his hands, swaying like a sapling in a hurricane. "Please. I'm unarmed."

"What are you doing here?"

The others are coming.

Smart. His mate was brilliant....

"I have nowhere else to go." Patel's voice wavered.

"How the fuck did you get in?" He made sure he was between Patel and James, and he needed to keep the guy talking.

"I crawled up to the roof and broke the emergency door to the AC unit."

"Jesus." What the fuck? This place was like Fort Knox, and that was pure desperation.

Patel folded in half, blinking. "I think I'll sit down." He crumpled to his knees.

Kit and Mick rounded the corner first, stopping short, and Kit tossed his head. "Poison."

"Shit." Mick's nose worked. "Smell familiar?"

Kit nodded. "We need to get him in a bed. He stinks with it."

"No. Put him outside. Let him rot." Dylan's voice was hard, implacable. "He tried to kill my mate."

"And he might be able to tell us what's going on," Mick snapped. "Get him someplace we can isolate him. Lock him in."

"Someone needs to figure out how he got in." Rey murmured. "So the crocs again?"

"No—" Patel whispered. "No crocs. Alone. Please."

"No." Hank sighed. "On the roof, he said. Air conditioning unit."

"I'll secure it," Brock growled. "Welcome the fuck home."

"Come on, babe. A bear can always help in these kinds of situations." Locke let Brock precede him, but that big body was tense.

"I'm going back to my office to work." James was pale as milk.

"No." Hank grabbed him. "We all lock down. Mick, you got Patel?"

"I do, and I have a bear too." Mick nodded at Kit, which was a good point. Hell, someone said Kit had taken the head clean off one bad guy during their last big battle with the bad guys during Patel's reign of terror.

What the hell was Patel doing here?

"I can—"

"No, Hank is right." Mick gave James a stern look. "If he has been given the same poison, you don't need to be near him, and you need to get some rest. When we do get information from Patel, you'll be on call."

James' growl was deep and wild, and he pushed out of the chair and stumbled away, managing an almost reasonable stalk.

Hank used that to his advantage, leading James away from the staring team, wheeling the chair just in case.

"Breathe, mate."

"Don't tell me to breathe! My boss just sent me to my *room*!"

Okay, that shook the walls.

"He did?" Hank blinked, then laughed, which got him pounced, James pushing him against their apartment door.

"No laughing!"

"Why not, baby? This whole thing smacks of ridiculous." Hank knew his chuckles were almost hysterical more than real humor.

"Because—because—" James seemed to get impossibly heavy, face flattening out. "We were safe before this. It was *good*."

"Inside." He opened the door and half carried James into the apartment. "We've just got the best lead ever. We're going to figure this."

"That's why I was going back to work!" There was a desperation in voice.

"Baby, please." Hank held on, trying to get James to stop freaking out. "Is it the tiger? Brock?"

What was triggering James?

Was it the smell of the poison? He had to admit, he could barely smell it. Mick and Kit had known it right away.

Maybe it was having to bring Brock in. Maybe it was just idea of the crocs.

Those things seemed to wig everyone out. They had completely destroyed a building...

"Talk to me, James."

"We were okay, before Patel. No one was trying to kill us, break down the building."

"Well, I'm pretty sure he's not the driving force. Not if he's this expendable." Hank couldn't help it. His cop brain was always calculating.

"I know, but...I'm having a snit, goddamn it!" James threw up his hands, then stomped his feet a little, which was good to see, as much time as he'd spent in the chair today.

"Rar." He dragged James to the sofa. "Knock yourself out,

baby." They had a lot to learn about each other. If James wanted to rant, Hank would let him.

"I'm tired of being scared, goddamn it! I'm tired of worrying! I want to go outside!"

"I want that too." He stroked James' hip. "I get why you want to be at the computer, but we need to clear your head first."

"I'm so mad, mate. So fucking pissed off."

"I don't blame you. I'm one bad guy removed." And without this situation, he would never have met his mate, so he had to be a little grateful, though he would never say that to any of these guys who had been through so much.

"Yeah. Yeah, I hear you." And James did, because he came right to Hank, taking his hand.

"Hey, you have every right." Hank reeled James in for a kiss, because he needed to feel his lover against him, to count James' heartbeat.

I'm tired of being frightened, mate. I'm tired of running. This whole thing, from the first croc to the last ferret, has just been a nightmare.

We're going to end this. Find out who's behind it and take them down. Hank believed that with everything in him.

Swear it. That quiet desperation made him growl.

He took James' cheeks between his hands, staring into those eyes, which glowed gold now instead of green. "I swear."

A single tear escaped his mate, James' breath hitching in his chest. "Okay."

"Okay." He took a kiss, unable to bear seeing James cry. James was so strong, so fierce, that it was easy to remember how delicate he could be.

Hank hugged James close to him, murmuring love words and nonsense, rubbing their cheeks together. It didn't take long for James to relax, to begin to purr.

That was more like it. No panic, just trust. Care.

He felt huge, being able to offer this to James. Kind of on top of the world, despite all the weirdness.

James leaned into him, resting hard and letting him hold on. They just floated, and the next thing he knew, their kitty selves were out and the clothes were replaced by fur, both of them chuffing madly.

He got one paw on shoulder, focusing on grooming, smoothing out the heavy golden fur. James' heartbeat slowed, his breathing coming back to normal, and soon those eyelids were drooping over those green-gold eyes. James was the best mountain lion ever.

Yes. My mate. Sweet angel.

Thank you, Hank. For being here. James sighed. *I needed you, your strength. I felt... scared and awful.*

You dreamed me here, baby. I was made for you. He loved James so much it hurt, and he had no intention of going anywhere. None.

I did. James rolled over and stretched. *Tigers are big, you know?*

They are. The biggest of us cats, huh? Hank was relaxed in body, but his mind was still racing. Why had Patel come to Apex in the first place? Was it just another set up, or had they caught a big break?

Yes. I—Does it bother you, that I'm not? Big, I mean. I was the runt. James searched his eyes, that gaze so worried.

Honey, I'm a bobcat. You already seem big to me no matter what. We're perfect for each other. Their paws lay next to each other, and sure enough, James' was a bit bigger.

James was his—brilliant and dear, a good friend and a better lover. There was no way he'd trade James for anyone else.

Biological imperative, James teased.

But a good one.

James' purrs grew louder, buzzing between them.

That was the ticket. Hank curled in to snuggle hard, just wanting the contact. They needed to regroup. Kit could sit on the tiger for a bit. And they had the grizzly.

And Dylan.

Dylan might be able to take—nah.

Then again, Dylan had some *rage*. Who knew what he might could do? And Locke was here now. Two bears could take a tiger. Especially one as broke-dick as Patel seemed right now.

He chuffed, thinking if anyone deserved a little debilitating drug action, it was that asshole.

James head-butted him, but it was less violent and more teasing. He could hear sweet laughter in his head, James playing with him. Thank God. That panic had been real. He'd never been the one who was trusted, that soothed.

You make me happy.

He hummed. *I usually hide in the shadows. You give me light, James.*

James groomed his feet, then moved up his leg to smooth his chest. It was heaven, to be loved on so well. Grooming was like... this luxury thing. Hank did it. All cats did in cat form. But to have a lover help? That was a warm fuzzy his world-weary cop self could hardly realize.

That's why we have each other—to have something that isn't work. James was focused on making him boneless.

Mmmhmm. Have each other. His brain was finally slowing down. Maybe he'd been a little battle ready too. He had to protect his mate, but he never got all flitter-pated until the emergency was over.

Mmm...pretty. James was melting him.

You too. Really. They were just basking, but they needed this time.

James gnawed on his ear in thanks, then straightened the tuft.

He batted at James with his paws, playing a little, but totally lazy and not meaning anything serious. God, this was fun.

James hugged him, the strong leg muscles bunching up around him. That felt amazing, so good.

They finally dozed together, and Hank knew they would come crashing back to reality soon, but now was for them. Only them.

He needed it, and he intended to keep it.

NINE

James woke up naked and human, curled around Hank and hanging on for dear life. God, seeing Patel had been a shock, his blood running pure ice in moments.

Hank was a grounding rod, though, and now he felt like he could go see what Brock had accomplished, what needed to be done.

Find out why they hell Patel was here.

More importantly, find out if his friends—Brock and Rey both—were all right. He hated thinking they were as frightened as he was.

Rey had to be out of his mind, in fact, and Dylan had been deadly angry.

He eased out of Hank's arms.

"Where y' goin'?"

"To check on Brock and Rey."

"Want me to come?"

"Give me about ten or fifteen?" He knew Brock, at least, was still a little up in the air about Hank.

"I'll be there in ten, mate." Hank brushed his thigh, loving on him. "I love you."

"Love you too." He did. So much it filled him from his toes to his head. He grabbed his crutches instead of his wheelchair, and he headed out, moving more and more easily.

Hank was loving the poison and weakness out of him, he was convinced.

"*Irmão*! Look at you!" Brock met him at the elevator. "I had to put Griz to bed."

"Is he all right? Are you?" He stood tall, proud of what he had accomplished.

"We're okay. This whole thing is weird and, how do you say? Smelly."

He chuckled. "You mean it stinks."

"Yes! That's it." Brock came to rub cheeks with him. "Where is your mate?"

"Getting dressed. He'll be here shortly." Brock smelled like family. "Breakroom?"

"Sounds good. Mick and Kit are watching over our... guest." Brock's nose wrinkle couldn't be more eloquent.

"Better them than Dylan, right?" Dylan had rage.

"Dylan would kill him, and we need information," Brock said flatly. They made it to the breakroom, and Brock looked around. "This place misses Carrie's touch."

James sighed. "She couldn't chance her family. Her mom. She said she'd come back if—" James cut off. If they got their shit figured out. Carrie was a fine admin, but she was no fighter.

"I don't blame her. Not at all. I almost didn't come back. We were goofballs on vacation."

"Were you?" He grinned, then eased into a chair while Brock grabbed them drinks. "What did you do?"

"Fucked. A lot. Every so often we'd groom or soak in a tub, but mostly fucking." That was so blissful.

James laughed. "Hell, we've been doing that, and we didn't have to go anywhere."

"*Sim*, well, you have less privacy. Griz and I destroyed furniture." Brock winked before handing him a Sprite. "I know I left you all in the lurch. It was too much, though. You were so sick, and I wasn't all there, and it was just—"

"No, I get it now." James did understand, because it *was* too much. All of it. "One of these days Mick is going to lose all his marbles."

"That is assuming a lot, to think he has any, hmm?" That made them both laugh like loons, which sure enough, drew another member of the team in.

Rey poked his head in the door. "Can I come in? Dylan is all growly, and I'm letting him pace outside the room where Mick and Kit have Patel."

"Come on, foxy." Brock held out a hand to Rey, who slipped in to take it, humming. No one wanted to be frozen out.

"Who wants a snack?" James said. "None of us are Kit, but surely we have salty potatoes in frozen form or something." They couldn't go wrong with fries or potatoes.

"We have tater tots," Rey agreed. "Let me toss some in the oven."

Food was their great common denominator. They bonded over it, showed love with it. All of them. "Hank will be along too."

"I'll make enough for all." Rey gave him a sweet grin, then got busy pulling tots out of the freezer and arranging them on a tray.

"I'll make something spicy to dip in." Brock's eyes danced, and James knew he wasn't in trouble. "I'm going to electrify the roof."

"That will kill the birds and leave one hell of a mess, brother," James pointed out.

"It might at that. But no one else will come in that way." Brock was struggling to keep a straight face, the laugh lines digging in around his eyes and mouth.

"Aren't you two cats? You could eat the birds..." Rey's eyes were twinkling.

"Pre-fried and all," James agreed.

"Singed feathers tickle my sinuses." Butter wouldn't melt in Brock's mouth.

"I like eggs better," Rey said cheerfully, making them both laugh.

"Is this where we sing 'Egg-Sucking Dog'?" he teased.

"I am a fox, thank you," Rey said in a lofty tone. "And I never steal them these days. I buy cage free."

"Foxes." Brock growled slightly, but he knew the man adored Rey.

"We're not all bad, anymore than all wolves are nice. Right?"

"Exactly." James grinned. "And god knows cats can suck."

"We bite," Brock agreed. "Hard."

"And leave all sorts of stuff behind."

"You guys are too full of innuendo." Hank swept in to kiss him. "What smells good?"

"Mmm...tater tots." James loved those kisses, that hunger. Hank made him want all sorts of things. Mate things.

"Totchos," Rey murmured over chuckles from Brock.

"Ooh...sour cream?" Hank asked, eyes wide.

"Uh-huh. And melty cheese."

"Damn. I'm in kitty heaven." Hank rolled his eyes and smacked his lips.

"Salty goodness," Brock agreed with a straight face. "That's what really makes guys like us happy."

They all looked at each other, eyes glowing in concert, even Rey, who was way more kitty than pup.

Hank hooted. "Be right back, okay?"

He nodded, figuring Hank was going to check on Mick and Kit. The man didn't like dangling loose ends at all. Dylan didn't either, so it had to be a cop thing. Tick all the boxes.

James looked at Brock. "We're okay? I mean, I know you didn't want to come back."

"I'm right as rain, *irmão*. I swear. We're a team, *não*? We can't stay apart long." Brock nodded firmly, emphasizing the words.

"We are. A pride." The weirdest, most wonderful pride ever. Such a misfit group, but stronger together than apart.

"Maybe a pack, if you ask Mick." Rey was always so quiet, but so determined.

He always knew how to say something without pissing anyone off. Which, considering Brock's temper, was something else.

"Yeah. A family. My family." Brock hugged Rey with one arm, squeezing him up against that strong, lean body.

Rey smiled, the expression so happy that James had to laugh with joy.

Hank came back in, looking a little frowny.

"What?" James asked, worried that something had gone wrong.

"Huh?" Hank shrugged. "Nothing. Patel is still asleep. I was hoping he'd be stirring like a loud little mouse by now. I'll take the guys some food when it's done so they can have a bite without leaving their post."

"You'll take some to Dylan, too?" Rey asked.

Hank winked. "He said he'd be along here. He likes tots."

"Are they sure?" James asked. "I mean that he's in there, asleep?"

"Yeah. Yeah, Kit keeps going and poking him. Hard. In the face. I think he might end up bruised a little." That kinda made Hank look... gleeful.

"He looks tiny," Brock muttered. "Not scary or dangerous at all right now."

"He's not tiny. He's evil." Rey looked totally stressed the fuck out.

James couldn't blame him. This was bringing on the worst kind of PTSD.

"I know." James pulled Rey to him for a hug. "It's okay. We're just using him for information. Then he can go back to jail."

"Why did he come here, James? When he could have gone anywhere? Why did someone kill the guard and set him free, only to have him come here?"

"I don't know? Maybe he had to? The poison? We did recover from it."

"Maybe." Brock scowled. "Maybe someone was driving him here."

"You ready to tell us what you know that we don't?" Hank drawled, staring at Brock.

"I'm not sure of anything. I can't— As far as I know, the only single person I can think of who could do all this is dead."

James met Brock's gaze. He knew more about Mal than the rest of the team, about the torture and fury and wild emotional bullshit that had happened, but that was a deep-held secret.

Hank's eyes narrowed, and James knew he was about to ask hard questions again. "Are you sure?"

"No. Dylan looked into it for me after the poisoning. There's a death certificate."

"I have a bunch of those for undercover jobs. So do you." Hank snorted. "What else do you have?"

"Not much. He had fifteen addresses. None panned out." Brock was looking a little hunted again, but James didn't think Hank was to blame.

"Why is he—"

"Let me see him!" The roar was huge.

They all whirled toward the door, Hank putting James behind him, Brock doing the same for Rey.

"He's talking about me." Rey and Brock spoke in concert.

Kit skidded into the room. "Patel wants to see Brock. I think— I think he's dying, Brock. We need to know what he knows."

Brock ran, and they all followed, a buzz wild of panic and urgency on the air.

James didn't realize he was on his feet and not in his chair until Hank swept him up, carrying him the last few yards. Patel was... god, the smell was awful, and he was drenched in sweat, his eyes almost glazed over with a white film.

Patel might have been an evil man, but no cat deserved to die like that. None.

"He's coming for you. He's got your attention now. And he'll be on full attack. He wants you. If you come to him, he'll leave the rest alone." Patel forced each word out, the tiger stripes shimmering on his face.

"Liar." Brock's snarl was true jaguar. "He'll never leave them alone."

"He?" Hank asked. "He who?"

"No. No way." He'd forgotten Griz was even there, with Kit and Mick, but that deep voice was panicked. "He's dead."

"He's—he's better at being bad than you are at being good. Everyone grab your things, separate, and run."

"No." Mick growled it out. "You tell us."

"Maldinado. He's alive. He's a vicious bitch. And he wants you." Patel leveled a shaking finger at Brock.

"You want us to just run?"

Brock grabbed Mick by the shirt front. "You don't get it! He'll kill all of you to get to me!"

Mick grabbed Brock right back. "He'll try."

A terrible gurgle came from Patel, and that big body arched, the air popping around them, the pressure immense. Then an emaciated tiger lay there, limp, all the life drained out of him.

Rey cried out, pushing into Dylan's arms, and James had to fight not to do the same. That was...so wrong.

Shit, that could have *been* him.

Hank grabbed his hand. "We need to call this in, Mick."

"Yes. Yes, we should. Do you have a contact? I don't want a ton of people trekking through here."

"I do." Dylan glanced at Hank. "You know Ty Grainger?"

Hank nodded. "I do. You take care of your guy. I'll call him."

"Take Brock and James with you. I worry that felines are more sensitive to this shit. Kit and I can deal." Mick shot Locke a wicked grin. "I'll let you decide where you go."

Griz snorted. "I'll go with the cats and be their bodyguard."

Dylan looked torn, but then gave Mick a wry glance. "Can I take—"

"Go. We got this." Mick's chin firmed up. "In fact, you all need to go to a safe house. I have a new one." Mick pulled out his wallet, then took out a slip of paper. "No one says it out loud."

Dylan took it, nodding. "We'll see you there in a few hours. Right?"

"No. No. No more safe houses. No more running." James couldn't do it again. He wanted to stay home.

"Then we fortify," Hanks said. "We take all but a few of the systems offline. Brock tells us EVERYTHING about this guy Maldinado. We need to work together."

"I don't want—" Mick started, but James shook his head.

"We've run and run. Nowhere is safer than here." James sighed. "We'll clear the hall, but we aren't leaving."

"Okay." Kit said it, and gave Mick a look when the boss would have protested.

"Shit! The tots." Rey struggled free of Dylan and ran back toward the breakroom.

Dylan followed at breakneck speed.

"I want you and the other felines in quarantine," Mick barked. "Now!"

James held up his hands. "Okay, jeez."

"Now!" That was a clear roar.

They fled, all of them hauling ass to the breakroom, which might not be the most fortified place, but it had tater tots and was centrally located. "Whose apartment?" James finally asked.

"Locke and I have the biggest," Brock said. "We have three bedrooms and a shitton of ammo."

"It'll be like camp," Hank teased. "Let's take the tots."

James nodded to Rey. "You and Dylan coming too?"

Rey nodded. "So long as I stay with Dylan, the rest doesn't matter."

"Well. Come on, *irmãos*." Brock led the way. "We just have to wait for the cops to leave."

Hank pulled out his phone. Right. He was supposed to be calling someone. Rey took James' wheelchair, and he looked back at the fox. "Thanks. You don't have to."

.

"I know. I want to." Rey bent to kiss the top of his head.

"Thanks, buddy. My hands appreciate it."

"It's been a tough day." Rey sighed. "We live in interesting times."

"No shit on that, man. I want boring."

Brock snorted. "Then you backed the wrong play. Wrong team, I mean."

"We were sort of boring before!" Which wasn't exactly true, but a cat could dream, right?

Dylan nodded. "That's why I quit being a cop and did

this. PI work is ninety percent sitting in a car and drinking coffee or surfing BeenVerified."

"See?" James teased.

"Dogs are lazy," Brock shot back.

"Oh, you bitch." Dylan said it with laughter in his voice, though. "You kits can nap all day, just moving from sunbeam to sunbeam."

"God yes." And he could just puppy pile together and hide, if he didn't have all this drama.

"Shh." Hank had gotten off the phone. "A few of the force are on their way. Discreetly. We can all just chill."

"It seems like we should be pushing..." James said. "We know who it is for sure."

"I meant about Patel," Hank said, rubbing a hand over neck. "The other, I think you're right."

That touch soothed him immediately, his body responding to his lover. He took one deep breath, then one more, trying to get enough air into his lungs, enough oxygen to his brain to think.

"Here we are." Brock's apartments were big enough for them all, and they settled together, falling on the food.

By the time they were done, they were all curled together in their favorite pile. Hank got yanked right in by Brock, which warmed James' heart. They breathed together, sharing space and air.

Being a pack or pride or whatever. It didn't matter what they called it. They were family.

They were family, together, and they were going to take this shit apart with claws and fangs and the power of all the brains they could put into it.

———

Hank's phone buzzed in his pocket, so he eased out of the nap pile, trying not to wake anyone. If nothing else, they were too cute.

The text simply said, <<Need you at the front>>.

Dylan slid out of the pile too, phone in hand. He jerked his head toward the door, and he and Hank slipped out into the hall. "Ty's here, I bet."

"Yeah. I'm not looking forward to this. At all." He shook his head and sighed.

"Me either." Dylan sighed. "This is gonna be a prayer meeting, I bet."

"Yeah, I can see that." Hank winced. As a former cop, he knew how police and city officials started to react when one person or group started to leave death and destruction in their wake on a regular basis.

"So, we deal with this in house. Any more bodies—"

"There's just going to be one more body." Hank wasn't sure of the details, but this fox had poisoned him and his mate.

"Yeah. Hell, yeah, I like the way you think." Dylan approved, his low growl satisfied.

"I'm a bastard, but you guys are my family now."

They grinned at each other, then sobered as they made their way down to the main entrance of the building.

"What the fuck is going on here, guys?" Ty growled, the sound deep and low. "How many goddamn bodies are we supposed to ignore?"

"Hey, your penal system lost him," Hank said, not backing down an inch. "Not something we did. We didn't kill him either. Whoever poisoned him did."

"But y'all sure as shit weren't on the goddamn phone as soon as he showed, were you?" Lord, that man could make some noise.

Lions. What were you gonna do?

"No. He had something to tell us." Dylan never batted an eye.

"You have a personal stake in this. You all do." Ty waved his hands, looking about ready to explode.

Dylan curled his lip. "Back off, man."

"It's true."

Hank scowled. "Look, man, we called you because you're one of us. You don't want to help? Fine. Then send us some asshole just out of the academy."

"Fuck off, buddy. I just want my life back. I want to be safe," Dylan growled.

Ty pursed his lips, staring from one of them to another. "Show me the tiger."

Mick appeared, some surgical masks in hand. "Kitties have to mask up, just in case."

"You think that it's worse for us? Seriously?" Ty looked shocked.

"I do. It hasn't affected the rest of us at all second hand, but some of the cats have been on the verge of death. And Patel is enormous."

"It laid him low, man." Dylan said it quietly, buy sincerity rang in his voice.

"Okay. I need to call the quarantine crew. We can't—guys, we can't risk all the felines."

"Okay." Mick agreed readily, which made Dylan and Hank both stare at him. "What? I'm willing to cooperate. But I need to know that anyone coming in is above being bought."

"No one's above being bought," Ty sighed. "But some of us are way more expensive than others."

"Good thing." Hank stopped himself from growling. Ty was a good guy, if a stickler for rules sometimes. "Just call in people you trust?"

Ty nodded sharply. "Is everything contained now?"

"Kit is watching the room Patel is in," Mick said. "The rest of the team is quarantining."

"Good deal." Ty led him and Dylan away from the others. "Y'all, we have to put a lid on this, or the normals are going to start fussing. What the fuck is the deal?"

"We're just starting to figure it out. There's an old... what?" Hank looked at Dylan.

Dylan crossed his arms over his chest. "An old business and personal associate of our team member Brock. He used to do black ops. The guy is targeting us to get to him, we think."

Oh, nice. Way more concise than Hank would have been. And way lighter on the personal details.

"A—are you serious? What the actual fuck?"

"I guess the guy after us is nuts?" Hank spread his hands. "We're still learning the sitrep."

"Just what I need. A lunatic shifter. Fucking A." Ty rolled his eyes, growling under his breath. "Half the damn department thinks we're all unstable already."

"Right?" Dylan clapped Ty on the shoulder.

"Let me make some phone calls. I need to get this put to bed. Can the bears wash everything down?"

"I'll help Kit," Mick growled.

"No. I need you."

Hank nodded. "I'll ask Locke. Kit doesn't need to deal with this alone."

"No. No, he doesn't. Kit isn't—" Mick growled.

Dylan chuffed softly. "He's solid as a rock, Mick. He'll be fine. Locke will help."

"Get Locke." Mick looked like a thundercloud.

Hank scooted to do just that, knowing Mick only had so much time before explosion.

James looked up as he came in. *Is it bad?*

It's not good. "Griz? Ty wants to keep the cats away from

the poison and get a team in here. He was hoping you could help Kit sanitize."

"Sure." Locke put one hand on Brock's dark head. "Please, mate. Stay here and safe. Watch Rey and James."

"I will. I promise. Come back soon." Brock stropped against that big hand for a second, purring.

"I will, I swear. I need you." The low rumble even made Hank smile.

"I hate just sitting here," Hank grumbled. "Can't you put us on Facetime?"

Locke blinked. "Sure."

James chuckled. "Facetime? I've corrupted with the technology."

"I want to see this, but no one will let me go." Hank winked. Damn it, he needed to see Patel, see what had happened.

"Well, not if you're going to get sick again."

"I know."

"Set up a tablet, James. I'll hook you guys up." Locke headed out, and they all grinned at each other.

"He's a good mate," Brock murmured.

James' eyes fastened on Brock, so serious. "He makes you happy."

Hank felt a niggle of jealousy, the slightest burn, and then James smiled.

"Not as happy as I am, of course."

Brock bared his teeth. "Of course."

Hank laughed, and Rey just gave them a smug smile. "Nah. I have the best mate ever."

"Woof." Brock's single word was filled with laughter.

Rey blew Brock a kiss, which had them all laughing but Hank, and he was fiddling with the iPad to get it set up. He wanted to see what he could see. He got the guys trying to relax, release the tension, but no. He needed answers.

Then they could all relax, once the bastard after them was taken down and no one else was going to get poisoned.

Brock came over to him, waiting in that silent, still way he had. It would be unnerving if he hadn't been undercover for so long. You turned on your lizard brain with that kind of work.

Maybe not your croc brain...

"He tried to break me. He shot me full of neutrinon and nobenime."

Hank blinked hard at Brock, his shock too big too contain. "Jesus."

Yes, mate. A shift-inhibitor and a drug that erases the will. Can you imagine?

No. Christ, what kind of asshole does that to someone who's supposed to be your mate?

Brock nodded. "He seduced me away from my true mate. Made me feel like the only man in the world. The smartest operative. The best looking. The best. Then he set about tearing me to shreds for fun, I think."

Rey had clapped both hands over his mouth, but now he whispered, "Or because he cared about you and he hated that."

"He doesn't care about anyone, Fox. Not anyone but himself." Brock's voice was bitter as ice, and Hank resisted the urge to reach out to him. Brock didn't need that. At least not from him.

Brock needed them all to be mad as hell and ready to go track this fucker down and chew him to pieces.

How can we do this, Hank? Seriously? What do we do?

We start small and work our way up. This guy may be our Moriarty, but even he went off a cliff.

And he took Sherlock with him.

Maybe so, but Sherlock only had Watson. They had a team.

A team that was damn sick of being knocked down. They had information now. They could do this.

The laptop rang, and he answered, Locke's fuzzy face showing up. "Let's do this. Are you recording?"

"We are... now." Hank hit the button. "Go."

"So, Mick had gone through his pockets before he went all tiger, and there was nothing. I got to tell you, though, even the cat is beat to hell. Looks like maybe electrical burns."

"Why pull him out to torture him?" That made no sense.

"Did Mal take his balls?" Brock asked. "That was his signature, back in the day."

"Shit. Help me roll him," Locke said.

The damage was obvious with Patel in cat form, unclothed, and it was nauseating. Hank swallowed back bile.

Brock nodded. "So we know. I know. I fought him before, broken and lost and alone. I'm none of those things now."

"You have us." Rey said it quietly, putting a hand on Brock's arm.

"Ty, your team needs to check him for electronics and shit," Hank said. "He doesn't need a tracker. Fucker knows where to find us, but we need to make sure he's not gonna explode or something."

Last thing they needed right now was an explosion. Shit, the last thing they needed right now was this. But they had it didn't they? They would take it on and win this time.

Brock bared his teeth. "That sounds like him. *Dios*."

"Get the body out," Ty ordered. "Now. Let's move it out. Fuck waiting for the containment team. Get it in a truck!"

Kit didn't hesitate. He hoisted the tiger carcass, and the vid went down at that point, Locke running to get the door.

Shit. Hank rose, but Dylan pulled him back down. "No. Don't make them worry about getting past you."

Brock roared, the fury ringing in the room, and Hank felt his mate's panic, fueling the emotions flooding the apartment.

They waited, the screen they'd been watching going blank. Ty would be calling the bomb squad, right? Shit. Hank vibrated, feeling utterly helpless, but Dylan was right. They would be in the goddamn way.

Think tactics. Come on. You're a fucking cop, man. The thought firmed his lips. "Let's move deeper in the apartment. Somewhere with no windows."

James, love? Can you check for bugs? Quietly?

Yeah. Yeah, I have my laptop. It can access the entire security system.

Good deal. Hank suddenly felt more like a border collie than a bobcat, herding everyone back to an inside bedroom with no outside access.

James tapped quickly and quietly, then Rey leaned in, nodded, and the fox's fingers started flying.

Good deal. He looked at Brock, who was gonna have a meltdown, then Dylan. "What else can we do?"

"Wait. I'll put the mattress over the door."

"They're moving him. Griz is coming."

"What about Mick and Kit?" Dylan asked, eyes beginning to glow.

"Griz says they were staying to help."

"They're our pack, damn it."

"Dylan, get the shower running. Brock, no touching your mate until he's decontaminated some."

"On it." Dylan headed for the bathroom while Brock snarled and paced, his metaphorical-at-this-point tail clearly lashing.

Hank just stared. Brock was far from all growl and no bite, but this was just stress. Lots of it.

We've got no bugs here in this apartment. There's a possible in the hallway, but I'd have to go out there to know for sure.

Not yet. We're not out of range, possibly, but we're close. It will be hard to get us in here.

We'll stay put. I want the body gone.

Me too. All the way gone.

"Nothing has exploded. Yet." Brock said. Yeah, he had a mind meld with Locke.

"That's handy. I'm basically opposed to explosions." Rey was gray, eyes still and stressed.

"No shit, *irmão*." Brock snorted, his voice dripping with irony.

James chuckled softly, nudging Rey with one shoulder. "We're going to make it right."

"I brought this here." Rey said, agony in his tone.

Brock snorted. "No, that was me."

"Well, I let him in." Rey gave Brock an anguished look. "I'm sorry."

"He wanted in, Fox, so he found a way. If not you, it would have been someone else."

"But—"

Brock reached out to snag Rey and hug him tight. "You're our family now, huh?"

"Stop mauling my mate, you bastard," Dylan teased. "Shower's running. Is he here?"

A knock sounded at the door, Locke's deep voice rumbling.

"I'll let him in," Hank said.

"I got it. All of you stay back," Dylan barked.

"He's pretty good at that," James chuffed, and Rey rolled his eyes.

"You have no idea."

Locke swept right through, Dylan on his tail, and the door slammed behind them. Dylan would get Locke's clothes bagged.

Brock paced, no doubt waiting for Locke to let him know it was okay.

Dylan came back out with a trash bag in hand. "Go on, jaguar."

Brock growled and nodded, running in to be with his mate.

Dylan kept motoring right through. "No one follows me yet."

"Not even me?" Rey stood, nose twitching.

"No. I'll be back, baby. I want you to stay in here." Dylan gave Rey this look that had them all blushing a little.

"I hate this," James whispered. "But I'm glad we're together. I'm glad we know who we're fighting."

"We're going to do this," Rey said, his chin lifting, copper eyes flashing. "We'll deal."

"We will." Hank knew this team had it in them. Shit, more than that, he knew his mate had this in him. They had a life to explore.

<<No bomb>> came the text from Mick. <<You can check for bugs now.>>

"Come on, babe." He smiled at James. "Let's check the hallway."

"Let's go. I want it done."

Hank wheeled James out, his mate searching electronically for listening devices. They checked, but who knew whether Patel had left bugs?

The whole situation was fucked up. They needed to hunker down and make a plan once the cops were all gone.

Funny, wasn't it, how fast they went from his co-workers to 'cops'.

A lot of them were great guys.

Apex Investigations was family now, and he intended to keep it intact. No matter what he had to do.

TEN

James sat at his computer, his fingers flying. He had a name now. He had a name and an MO and a fake webpage that had to have a backdoor in it so he could find out where this ex of Brock's was hiding.

Fucking asshole, attacking the cats specifically. It was like throwing a dart and just hoping he hit Brock. Not that it would matter if he did only get their resident jaguar. Brock was James' brother in arms. His pride. He would protect the man with his life.

Or in this case, his knowledge.

He typed and typed, watching code run on the screen, working faster that way than he did in a Windows or even Mac IOS.

"Very Matrix," Rey said softly from behind him, making him jump.

"I thought everyone else was asleep," James breathed. "Shit, you scared me."

"Where's Hank?" Rey looked exhausted, bags under his eyes, lines carved around his mouth.

James sent a tiny tug to their bond. "He *is* asleep."

"So is Dylan. Dealing with all that wore him out."

Chuckling, James nodded. "His rage burned bright, Foxy."

That made Rey grin. "I know. He's something else, my wolf. My protector."

"He loves you something fierce." A few months ago, that would have caused James a pang of sadness. Now he had a mate, and he didn't have to pine for something he worried he would never find.

"You're not sitting in your wheelchair!" Rey bounced, gaze going from him sitting in his gaming chair to the wheelchair sitting in the corner of the room.

"Nope. My muscles are screaming, but I'm trying to start doing as much normal physical stuff as I can."

"Oh, I'm so happy." Rey kissed his cheek. "Wanna come watch a horror movie marathon with me and Kit later? He's wigged and he just doesn't want to admit it."

"Only if we can watch *Rose Red*." That silly Stephen King mini-series made him stupidly happy. One of the things Hank was teaching him, slow but sure, was how to take downtime again. Work was important. Beating this enemy of theirs was crucial. But mind and body both needed rest.

"We can even watch the original *It* mini-series."

"You are speaking my retro language." He gave Rey a soft smile. "Want to help me out for a bit? I'm back-tracing the dummy site Mal hooked up to watch us. I could really use your help hunting down any and all public information you can find about Brock. You don't know him as well, so you'll have a fresher perspective."

Rey slid into his chair, his work face on, expression serious. He cracked his knuckles. "I'm in."

They both got to work, the nerve center of Apex Investigations alive with tapping keys, soft dings, and *blinking* cursors.

They were together. That was what mattered.

———

Hank woke with a start, his dream a 3D, smell-o-vision replay of what had happened over the last forty-eight hours. His heart pounded, and he reached for James, frowning when his mate wasn't in bed with him.

So he sent a little thought toward James, trying not to panic. The place was on high alert. Someone would have gotten him if something else had gone wrong. *Angel? You okay?*

Been working. I'll be there in a few?

I'll be waiting. It was gratifying that James would come to him rather than keep working when he knew James wanted this situation fixed, solved, and sealed in a paperwork tote in the basement.

He grabbed his phone, noting a text from an unfamiliar number. The texts always had the same area code, though, and they always just said the same thing. <<Check in>>.

Yay.

He hit call on the number, waiting for his Bureau handler to answer.

"'Bout time you checked in," was what he got by way of greeting.

"I was told you had approved the action I was on." Hank actually kind of liked Special Agent Cole Matthews pretty well. "Am I wrong?"

"No. You coming back?"

Hank blew out a breath. "Fuck no. I can tell you who was pulling Hetrick's strings. That ought to buy me out."

"Who?" Matthews barked.

"His name is Joao Maldinado. Fox shifter."

"Jesus fucking Christ, DeLong. You guys don't play around."

"You know him?"

"He's a ghost. A legendary one." Matthews rumbled. "Okay. I'll process you out, and clear with upstairs." Cole paused. "I'll also send a few guys I trust to keep an eye on your little PI agency. I have a feeling you'll need them."

Shit. "Thanks, man. I'll owe you one." It could be nice to maintain access to Matthews's task force while they dug in against this fox guy.

"I know. That's why I'm doing it."

The line clicked off, and he was still staring at his phone, his brain just not quite moving fast enough to deal with all this shit, when James walked into their bedroom.

"Hey." James walked behind his wheelchair, looking strong. And concerned. "What's up?"

"I just quit my job."

"Wha-at?" James' voice rose, those green eyes flashing gold. "You just started! You can't!"

"Huh? No, my undercover job, baby." He grinned at James' immediate shamefaced relief. "My handler texted me, so I called it in. I'm a full-time Apex man now."

"Oh, my God." James rushed over and thumped down on the bed. "You scared the stuffing out of me."

"Sorry, angel. Really." He reached over to grab James' hand. "I just figured now was the time. I need to be able to focus on you, and on my job here."

James twined their fingers together. "I don't hate it."

"My old boss has heard of Brock's ex. Some kind of shadow legend."

"Yay." James rolled his eyes. "So is he going to help us?"

"Surprisingly? Yes." Hank had to grin. "Though I'll owe him a favor."

Growling, James pushed him down on the bed, then straddled him and tossed his phone aside moments later. "I'll bite him if that involves you leaving for any length of time."

"Hey, my money is on you. Always." He grabbed James' ass, sad that it wasn't bare.

"Yeah?" James kissed him, hard enough to sting a little. "Good."

"I'm not leaving you again, James. Last time I was thinking it was all a fevered drug dream. This time I know better. I love you."

Hank drew back to stare into his eyes, that green gaze a little damp. "I love you too. Thank you for being my dream man, Hank. You saved me. I love you too."

They shared another kiss, then another and Hank didn't feel tired and beaten down anymore, no matter how bad an enemy they might be facing.

He had James. He could face anything that came his way.

Epilogue

"Goddamn it, Mick, what the hell is going on down there? Dead tigers after they jailbreak? Dire crocodiles? Bomb squads and hazmat?" His contact higher up in the police force, Captain Greg Douglas, was shouting at him, really reading him the riot act.

Mick was too damn tired to care.

"Look," he said, cutting Greg off. "We've had a shit time if it. We've been targeted, and I refuse to take the blame for this crap."

"Tell me what's going on, man. I can help."

"One of our team members used to do black ops. When he retired, he had an enemy who's held a grudge. All of this stems from him." The fucking bastard was named Joao Maldinado, and Mick would chew him to pieces with his wolfy teeth if he ever got to actually lay eye on the asshole.

"Jesus." He heard Greg chewing on a toothpick. "What can we do to get this guy?"

"I don't know." He was starting to wonder if they should just... disband. They could be safer if they scattered, but that would leave Brock in the wind. Mick couldn't do that, not after what Maldinado had done to him. Besides, these guys were his fucking pack. "I need your resources. James needs your databases."

"Shit. You're asking a lot, but this is my city, and I'm sick of this dick destroying shit."

"Us too." Mick walked the halls, his earpiece in one ear, the other cocked so he could check on his sleeping team. The hazmat crew had cleared the building, they'd done a full surveillance sweep, and they'd locked down the fucking danger areas on the roof. How could someone have gotten in the building. Someone as big as Patel?

"You got what you need, Mick. Just don't lose me my job."

"Thanks, Greg. Thanks for stepping up. I swear, this guy makes me feel like an amateur, and you know me."

"I do. We'll get ahead of this. Have you thought about a safe house?"

"I have several lined up, but last time we did that, it was a disaster."

"Okay. I'll put some of my guys, the shifters I trust, on watch at your place. Plainclothes."

"And I'll send you all I have on the last year of our damn lives."

"Good. Time we started working together."

Mick snorted. "I'm not to one who kept sending underlings and not calling."

"Shit. You suck, man." Greg chuckled. "Send that shit to me."

"I will." He hung up, then turned a corner to find Kit watching him from the doorway of his apartment.

"Cops getting involved?"

"Greg."

Kit nodded. "Ah. You hungry?"

Mick started to say no, but Kit looked so... alone. Sad. So he nodded. "Sure, kiddo."

Kit turned, leading him inside. "I'm not a kid, you know," Kit snapped, never even glancing at him.

Mick paused, staring. He called Kit that all the time. "I know that."

"You always treat me like one unless you need my bear. I'm not useless, and I'm not a freaking child like I was when you found me." Kit moved to the kitchen, rattling dishes, his wide shoulders stiff.

Mick stood there, staring, wondering if maybe he should just shoot himself. That might make life easier.

Instead, he went for something he didn't do so great. Listening. He followed Kit into the kitchen, tugging out a chair when he got there. "Okay, tell me what you want me to call you, Kit."

End

Want More?

Join the Spurs and Shifters Newsletter for free stories, news, and contests from Julia Talbot and BA Tortuga!

https://lp.constantcontact.com/su/A9CRUzp/baandjulia

Afterword

Hey, folks!

Thanks so much for reading my book! I'm so glad you made it here. If you liked the book, I hope you'll consider leaving a rating or review at your retailer of choice or adding the book to your Goodreads shelf.

If you're interested in more of my books, or in news about when they come out and what's coming soon, please check out my Facebook Group https://www.facebook.com/groups/juliatalbot/ or my newsletter here: https://lp.constantcontact.com/su/A9CRUzp/baandjulia

XXOO and Keep reading!

Julia Talbot

Also by Julia Talbot

Alpha Tales

An Alpha in Sheep's Clothing

Packmate for Hire

Too Many Alphas

Apex Investigations

Fox and Wolf

Jaguar and Grizzly

Mountain Lion and Bobcat

Alpha and Bear

Apex Security

Solids and Stripes

Dead and Breakfast

Fangs and Catnip

Fangs for the Memories

Home for the Howlidays

Full Moon Dating

New Moon

Isaiah and Jameson

Grizzly List

Bear Wanted

One and Only Bear

Bearly Working

Midnight Rodeo

Big Bear, Little Bear

Light a Rocket

Vampire Protection

The Dragon's Dilemma

Up in Flames

Nose to Tail, Inc.

Wolfmanny

Wolf's Man Friday

Wolf Maneuvers

The Peculiars

The Curse of the Mummy's Heart

The Shadow of the Count

Riding Cowboy Flats

Jackass Flats

Just a Cowboy

Riding the Circuit

Summit Springs

High Side

* * *

Contemporary

Catching Heir

Chef on Chef

Drive Your Truck

Home for the Hollandaise

Jumping, Landing, and Taking

Loose Snow

Love Dot Com

One More Yule Log

Out of the Frying Pan

Perfect

Sparkle and Shine

Historical

A Gentleman of Substance

A Pirate's Paradise

Offerings

Partners on the Trail

Post Obsession

Remembering Pleasure

To Hell You Ride

The White City

Paranormal

Bad Dog

Blue Moon Bar

Faster Bobcat

Link to the Crescent

Night of the Living Manny

Pack Mates

The Fire Inside

Thorns

Tomb of the God King

Touching Evil

About the Author

Julia Talbot lives in the great Southwest with her wife and four basset hounds. A full-time author, Julia writes paranormals and more with lots of love and action and, as her alter ego Minerva Howe, she writes mpreg and alpha/omega stories. She believes that everyone deserves a happy ending, so she writes about love without limits, where all of her stories leave a mark.

Visit Julia's website: http://www.juliatalbot.com